SILVERS

HOLLOW

PATRICK DELANEY

For Kaylin

"It's no use going back to yesterday, because I was a different person then."
Alice in Wonderland — Lewis Carroll

I wake at the foot of a metal step as the train pulls away. It's night. I lay still, a subtle throb in the back of my skull. The less I move, the less it hurts.

Strangeness has overtaken the hour. Something unexplainable is happening. It feels eerie, contrived.

I'm motionless, letting my memory calm, a storm of confusion swirling in my eyes. I can't hear the steel titan as it slips away from the platform, only feel the vibration it leaves in its wake. The noise returns as its bulk groans along the tracks, skating away into the black night.

I sit up, my muscles sore, overcome with an aching so

profound it hurts to breathe. My body tells me I'm beyond exhausted, as if I've spent an entire day hiking a treacherous mountain range but can't remember why.

I force myself to my feet and look around.

I recognize this place. I'm at the train station in Silvers Hollow, my childhood hometown. The *edge* of town to be more precise.

What am I doing at the train station? Was I leaving? Or coming home?

These questions carry a weight my body isn't equipped for. I try not to dwell on them, knowing they will likely come back.

I glance up at the sky, where I can make out nothing but a sea of blackness obscuring the stars. It seems different somehow. *Closer*, in a way. More urgent. There is a quality to the air that's not how I remember it. It's touched by nature; it smells like rain and wet earth. It's still. There's no breeze or wind. Everything is silent, frozen. Cold.

I'm the only one on the small concrete platform. A ghost of the woman I once was. The train depot is closed. Beyond the windows, nothing but shadows. Not a single leaf nor crumpled newspaper stirs around me. I'm all alone here, alone with my thoughts.

As the glowing red eyes on the rear of the train fade away, I can't help but note a swell of anxiety, as if I'm supposed to be on it. My instincts tell me that I'm not where I'm supposed to be. I trust them. This feels wrong. Being here feels wrong.

What am I doing back in Silvers Hollow? I thought I'd forgotten about this place, left it to rot.

My face is drenched in sweat, my bangs damp, as if I've just run a marathon. My throat is tickled by the air as I draw in a few deep breaths. It doesn't feel natural. It's thinner, artificial. No matter how hard I try, I can't seem to get enough oxygen to my lungs. Everything is damp. The humidity is off the charts.

I turn my head and the back of my skull screams with pain. I clench my teeth in agony, eyes winced, gently fingering a laceration on the back of my head.

My hands are filthy. My nail polish is chipped, and there's blood on my fingertips. It's dark, but the color is unmistakable. There is no moonlight that I can see, only a pale fluorescent light at the end of the platform. The lamp coats the platform in a melancholy, bluish glaze.

I hold my hand closer to my eyes. The blood on my fingertips looks even darker under that unsettling tint than it would normally.

Is this why I was lying on the platform? Did I pass out? Did someone hit me? Did someone do this to me?

I'm suddenly paranoid, self-conscious. I toss glances toward the ends of the platform, but it's no use. Even if there was someone standing there, I wouldn't be able to see them. Standing here on the platform in the dark makes me uneasy. I look across from the platform to the other side of the tracks.

A sheer wall of granite.

I sigh, as my eyes scale the wall. It's high. Only the bottom is visible, the rest merges with the night sky. Was this mountain here before? I struggle to recall memories from my childhood, but I can't. They're long gone.

I begin to step toward the depot when my boot kicks a folded piece of paper. I quickly spring to grab it, forgetting there's no sign of a breeze and feel a little bit silly.

The sudden movement causes the throb at the back of my head to reawaken. It punishes me with a hammer of painful knocks to my skull.

I gather the paper, folding open the edges to find it's an old photograph from my childhood. The picture is of Father, Mother, Ivy, and me. We're standing at the base of the gazebo in town square. Beyond that— the church. The sides of the picture are framed by dozens of old shops and restaurants. The photo has changed since the last time I saw it. The white trim around the edge is yellowed, the corners worn, the memory blemished with sharp white fold lines.

Why do I have this? I haven't seen this polaroid for over twenty years. I've never had it in my apartment, much less carried it in my wallet. So why do I have it now? I'm not sure why, but something tells me it's immensely important.

The photo draws me in, and my old life comes rushing back at me like waves of white, foaming water.

I admire the snap a moment longer before adding another crease to its aged surface, tucking it into my pocket for safe keeping.

It isn't long before a hollow bell rings out, drawing me around the depot to the front. I try to count the chimes as I hurry around the building, but I can't focus, and any chance I have of figuring out the time fades away.

The concrete stage turns to wooden planks. My feet thrum as I move along them to the facade, like I'm walking a town in the Old West.

The church bell continues, calling to me from the center of town. It's solemn, sad. Even more so in the middle of night. Depressing as hell. I remember that even when I was a kid it sounded like that. Strange for a place meant to bring hope.

It's at this point that I begin to wonder what time it is.

Remembering that I have a watch, I lift my sleeve to find that it's gone. I twist my wrist curiously, staring down at the pale strip of skin in confusion, checking the platform. Perhaps it fell off?

I retrace my steps. The bell's chimes cry out at the night sky like moans of the dead. After a full four minutes,

I abandon the search. My watch is gone. Lost, just like me.

I must have taken it off somewhere. Or did it fall off? I hate the idea of it lying somewhere in the dark, exposed. Alone. Is that dumb?

And just like that, my mind is racing for the train again, wishing myself onto it, reeling with a panic I can't quite understand.

Something tells me that I should have been on that train. And now it's gone.

"It's a good thing I found you when I did."

I'm in the back of a police cruiser, a thick mesh wire between the officer and I. It reminds me of the cages they keep animals in. It's suffocating. Primitive. How has the world come so far, yet it still relies on things like this?

The car isn't moving, mind you. We're just sitting in front of the train station. I spy the faint glow of his dated miniature computer and panel.

He believes me to have been loitering at the train depot. A ridiculous idea considering it was empty and I was alone. If he possessed any lick of sense, he'd know I'm not homeless.

I can't see him now and I couldn't see him then. He's veiled in convenient shadows, his face hidden from me. His voice is calm, in control.

I'm not under arrest per se, but I could tell by his reaction to finding me here, at the train depot, that he's irked. I don't know if it's due to his concern for my wellbeing, or because I've interrupted his routine. I'd guess the latter.

"It isn't safe out there," he says.

This comment strikes me as odd. Silvers Hollow is probably the safest place on earth. He's talking nonsense.

"No, sir, not safe at all," he repeats.

"I'm sorry," I say. "What are you talking about? Why?"

He draws in a deep breath, then exhales it at his dash. Even without seeing his face I can tell he's not as calm as he's making out. He's shaken by something. Rattled.

I wait for him to answer.

He ignores my question. "What were you doing out at the train station this time of night, young lady?"

"I'm sorry?"

"You been drinking tonight? Partying out there, at the station? Hell, I wouldn't blame you, night like this."

I have no response to this. Clearly this man isn't as smart as I would have believed.

"A night like what?" I ask.

"I think there's been a little mix-up about our roles here," he says, shifting on the leather seat. "I say again, what were you doing at the train station?" The calm in his voice is forced.

For some reason, I'm compelled to answer with the most obvious answer I can think of. "I was waiting for the train."

He breathes a laugh, cocking his head to the side. I see a jeweled blue eye in the shadow of mesh on his face. He turns back with a grunt.

"The train?" he says, skepticism in his tone.

"Yes."

He turns once more and gazes out the window at the façade of the train depot. A sad white trim frames the windows and awning. The doors to the inside are crimson red. A chill passes through me like a ghost.

"Where did you think you were going?" he asks.

I hang my head, sifting through my thoughts. I turn to look at those red doors again. The fresh coat of paint on them stands out. Even at night. It's dark, but the color still burns through the haze of confusion swirling around me. But wait—an experience from when I was younger springs out like a horrific Jack-in-the-Box. The doors were blue, weren't they? I've been at this train station before, back when Mother and Father sent me and Ivy to Winterview for the day. It was the first time we'd ever been allowed out on our own. We stood under that same awning and walked right through those two blue doors. But these are not the blue doors I remember. They're red, the color of an apple.

I can feel Officer Smith's gaze in the rearview mirror. He never offered his name, so I give him one. The most generic one I can think of. While he's calm, his eyes are intense, penetrating. They see through my lie clearer than a pane of glass. But there's something else in those eyes; an uncertainty, and a sadness.

I was right. Something strange is happening. I can't

pinpoint what it is exactly, but I know it to be true.

"This train hasn't run in decades," he says.

My breath hitches. "What?"

"The train; it hasn't run in over twenty years," he says matter-of-factly.

My eyes catch his in the mirror. "No, that's not right," I argue. "I saw it. It just left."

He shakes his head without even considering my words. "Afraid not. Lived here all my life, darlin'."

I find myself reaching for the bump on the back of my head, second-guessing myself. No. I know what I saw. There was a train. It was there. I saw it. The only question is: Why is he lying about it?

Officer Smith has decided to take a detour.

At this hour? Why? Especially with me in the car. The police station isn't in this direction.

I'm more than a little uneasy. I've seen this scenario play out in my head a thousand times. A woman on a dark road with a strange man.

Only it's never me. Never *my* face. Only other women. Other faces. Because you think it could never happen to you. Until it does.

I wonder: If I disappeared right now, would anyone notice?

The car rolls unsteadily through the night over an unpaved road. The rear window is cracked and the wind creeps in, throws sheets of the cold over my face. The air is drying out my eyes and I blink hard to try and wet them again.

The brakes groan like a subway car and we stop so abruptly that I pitch forward and nearly hit my face on the steel mesh dividing us.

"Hey," I shout. "What the hell?"

Officer Smith isn't fazed. He reaches out of view and comes back with a baton in his hands. The weapon seems unnatural there, and he stares at it long and hard, as if considering it.

Alarm sirens are firing off in my head and I catch his eyes in the mirror burrowing into me. A sense of panic starts to carve its way out of my stomach. I feel my pulse begin to rev up.

I hear the wood creak as his hands tighten around the club.

The realization is dropped into my lap that I'm alone, in the middle of nowhere. I'm unarmed, and I've foolishly trusted this stranger with nothing more than his word and a shiny piece of metal he hauls around with him. I have no control of what is about to happen, and I suddenly understand how easy it is to become lost in this world.

He throws open the door and the lingering mist rushes into the car. The chill sweeps across my skin and I feel a burst of adrenaline jolt my nervous system. I brace myself, mentally prepare for him to drag open the rear door. All the muscles in my body constrict and I'm shaking to pieces. I melt into the backseat like a puddle of water and squeeze my eyes closed. I listen as my heart swells and thrashes against my ribs, and all I can feel is a sickness in the hollow space where my stomach is.

There's a *thump!* and I hear footsteps on gravel.

My eyes peel open to find him moving away.

My clamoring nerves are shaken, but they begin to ease the further he walks away from me.

I watch him mosey through the dust-laden high beams. I can't explain it, but somehow, irrationally, as he passes through the cones of light, the shadow of a monster burns away and I see nothing more than a man. "Just stay there." His words echo over his shoulder to me, bouncing off the granite of the valley.

He continues up a small hill.

He stops at the top, bathed in the pale light from the headlights. He doesn't speak, and gets down on one knee. Where there is nothing, I envision a grave marker, like he's paying his respects to someone he knew once, a long time ago.

Growing impatient and slightly claustrophobic the longer I sit in this backseat, I decide to test my courage and find out what he's doing. Nobody should have to be alone tonight. As far as I can tell, he doesn't intend to harm me. He's had the chance. Plenty of chances. So I decide that he's not a threat. At least not right now.

"Hey!" I shout from the window. "What is it? What's going on?"

Officer Smith doesn't say anything, and as the silence sets in, I'm greeted by the lull of water. It's all white noise, gentle and soothing.

I push my face closer to the space above the window. The air is fresher than it was before. The same way the air is fresher at the beach than in the city.

The car door; it's unlocked.

I don't wait for permission.

He sees me coming and quickly gets to his feet. The flashlight beam cuts through the blackness and makes contact with my eyes and it's so blinding I'm surprised I don't faint. I throw my hands up defensively and jerk my face away.

"Do you mind?"

"I told you to wait in the car."

He doesn't try to stop me as I climb toward him, only keeps the funnel of light trained on me, like that will be enough to freeze me in place.

The sound of the running water grows in my ears and, as I step beside him, he holds out an arm. But it's not as if he's trying to restrain me. At least, not in an authoritative sort of way. It's more like he's protecting me from going any further. From hurting myself.

Even though it's dark out here in the forest, there's a tint to everything. You might think that color is a veil. And you'd be right. You have to look closely, but it's there.

Officer Smith and I stand side by side, shoulder-to-shoulder before a great fissure in the earth. And in that fissure is a vast river.

Officer Smith waves his light over the inky ribbon that cuts through the mountains, and it's swallowed up. I feel tiny patters brush against my cheeks and hear buzzing whiz past my ears.

We stand listening to the water and I look over at him. He can't seem to take his eyes off it.

Under the moonlight I see someone else standing before me. Officer Smith is gone. I can't see his face, but I hear him breathe. He's become someone from my past. Someone dangerous, and obsessed. I hear the calculated tick of a clock and a heavy whirl flutter past my ears.

While he's standing there, his back to me, the thought crosses my mind that I could push him. Watch him fall to his death and then take his car.

I wonder, am I the only one who has these types of thoughts?

But I don't.

Because this isn't him.

The rising anger melts away and I see Officer Smith again, perched on the cliff, two steps away from loose soil and his death. I slowly extend my hands and clutch handfuls of his coat in my hands, steadying him.

He cocks his head over his shoulder and smiles, then turns back to the water. It appears he's just as bad with trust as I am.

He holds the beam on the river long enough for his face to set in a frown, and then he lets the pale funnel fall to the pine needles scattered below our feet.

"Damn…" he says. There's distress in his tone, but I'm not sure why. Was he expecting to find something here?

"What is it?"

He studies my face for a moment as if he wants to let me in on the secret, then shakes his head, brushing the thought away.

"We need to go," he says.

He turns, and I peer back at the river to say goodbye to the fresh air, and as the flashlight skitters over the black water, I sense something enormous waiting below the surface, inevitable and vile.

An evil has come to Silvers Hollow.

S ilvers Hollow. A place for families. A place for friends and laughs and perfectly manicured lawns. Barbeques in the backyard with hot dogs and hamburgers and cold beer. Trivial pleasantries, banal conversations. Frivolous things, really. It's the sort of place where the sun always shines. Always.

Except tonight, of course.

So why can't I shake the feeling that there's something...*off* about this place.

The town is draped beneath a curtain of darkness. I try to look out the window at the night, but only find nothingness. The motion of the police cruiser is soothing.

It calms my shaky nerves.

Officer Smith hasn't said a word since we left the river. He's quiet, focused. I'm grateful. I don't know if I could handle any more lies tonight. He claims the train hasn't run in years, but I know what I saw.

Officer Smith eyes me in the rearview mirror but doesn't speak. I'm quiet too, as we drive. But only because I'm trying so hard to remember. To remember how I got here. To remember why I woke up on that platform, alone.

"Don't worry, everything is gonna be all right," he says.

I look up. I don't say anything, only watch his eyes in the mirror.

He shifts in his seat, talking out of the corner of his mouth. "So, um, how long has it been since you've been here?" he asks. There's apprehension in his tone, but I'm not sure why.

This question. A simple question, yet I can't find the answer.

"I, uh…"

There's a pinch between his brow, worry clouds his

eyes. "I remember you," he says, scooting forward in his seat. "You're his daughter, aren't you?"

I nod.

"Thought so," he says, raking a hand through his hair. "He'd be less than thrilled hearin' you were down at the old abandoned rail station this time of night."

I've never seen this man before in my life. He seems to know me, though. Somehow. There is something familiar about him. His mannerisms, his speech. It's all there, yet distorted somehow.

"What time is it?" I ask. My voice sounds pathetically weak, like a student afraid to speak up in a classroom.

I see his eyes narrow at the mention of the word "time." It's subtle, but it's there. He's not anymore a fan of it than I am.

"Hello?"

The man doesn't answer, simply keeps driving us to our destination. I want to ask, *where are we going? Am I under arrest?* But I don't. I'm too exhausted and my head is pounding. I feel an itch in my forearm and I scratch away at it like a lottery ticket.

Outside the car, wave after wave of trees pass before my eyes. I see dark crevices between the trunks, wondering what might be waiting on the other side, in the great beyond. Some trees rise so high I can't see where they end and the sky begins.

After my skin is raw and nearly bloody, I push back my other sleeve, feeling around my wrist.

Where is my watch?

I'm never without one. Even when I was little I wore one. A gift from my mother. I started out with one of those plastic neon-colored ones from the 80s and worked my way up as my income increased. Lately? A white gold Tissot with an alligator band. Most people nowadays believe a cellphone tells the time just as well. Not me. I don't trust them. A battery can die. A phone can break. The logic makes zero sense to me. What's more important than time? My father was the first to illuminate this concept. Time governs our entire lives, looming over us. It controls every aspect of life. You spend too much time on one thing, it eats away time from something else. It's common sense, and my watch is one of the few accessories I can't live without.

My jaw clenches. I pull down my sleeve to hide my irritation.

Up ahead, I see lights. They remind me of a carnival, pulsing with life. They begin as small, floating orbs in the distance, then gradually move closer.

And there it is. The sign. The welcome sign at the beginning of town. The white paint is stark against the night. There's something different about it.

The car slows, coasting now like a boat on the ocean being carried by the waves. The cruiser jumps onto the concrete.

The sign—the wood is new. It's not the rickety assortment of panels I remember from my childhood. There's no split boards. No peelings of paint. In fact, the white paint is brighter than I remember it. It's almost *too* white. It isn't the eggshell I remember with the sapphire letters and the fine blue border. All of the words are red now, just like the door from the depot. They must have repaired it?

It's the small things you notice most, I think. Before,

the sign was welcoming. The blue letters on the antique base reminded me of the ocean, as if Silvers Hollow were a coastal town. Hell, Winterview is closer to the ocean than Silvers Hollow. Why did they paint it red? The crimson letters bleed through the bleached white. It looks like someone painted the letters with a pint of blood. It's ugly, defaced. I almost would have preferred graffiti. At least that would have other colors. The townspeople must have thought it would be more eye-catching this way. I disagree. It's lost its charm, screaming for people to notice it.

I watch the sign pass by the side of the car. It disappears in the side mirror, lost to the night.

The Nighthawk Diner. A 50s dream that has been in Silvers Hollow for as long as I can remember. I love this place, always have.

For the kids raised in Silvers Hollow, the Nighthawk Diner was *it*. Legendary. Famous even, to outside towns and cities, maybe even countries! Once, it even made it to TV, if you can believe that. Some renowned chef made it his mission to come out and sample the special: The "James Dean." A bacon cheeseburger on a toasted pretzel bun so good you could die just from the smell alone.

I could always tell right when I was about to enter town, because the glow from Nighthawk's was much louder than the other lights in town. It's unique, almost eerie. From an outsider's perspective, seeing a glowing green light gradually appear in the woods could be unnerving. But to those of us who grew up here, it only brings smiles and hunger.

Silvers Hollow—a small town for small people. At least it was, from what I can remember. The town plaza isn't all that big. I think its humble size is part of its charm. There's a pharmacy, a coffee shop called Hallowed Grounds, Sally's Taqueria, a book shop, and the church, of course. All of it surrounds the town square, where in the middle there's a faded gazebo and perfectly trimmed strips of green grass. But now, everything looks so much cleaner—brand new, as if it's sprung up overnight.

Silvers Hollow has endless strings of bulbs that run along most of Main Street. They have this holiday quality about them. They make the town look like it's always Christmas, like it could be on a greeting card. I didn't mind seeing them everyday. Growing up here, I kind of liked it, actually. Maybe that's why they never took them down. Because they never wanted that feeling to go away. They wanted the town to stay timeless. Suspended. The world went on, but Silvers Hollow stayed behind.

But at Nighthawk's, there's a different kind of light. The energy here is different. It's...*electric*. Dangerous even.

My eyes grow wide as Officer Smith and I draw nearer.

And there it is. The same sputtering emerald sign that has been here since before I was born and will be here long after I die.

Officer Smith lowers my window a tad. *These* lights are different. *Nighthawk's* is different. Edgier. Its chromed accents mirror the town perfectly. The establishment is just how I remember it. You would probably assume that being a "retro-themed" restaurant would make this place stick out like a sore thumb, and it does. But not for the reason you would think. Nighthawk's is a place from the past that's, ironically enough, ahead of its time. I try to wrap my head around the idea. Is that even possible?

I peek through the long plate-glass window that runs the length of the façade. I can't make out much, but I see Lyle—the owner—inside. Relief washes over me. I'm surprised by how much better I feel just seeing one familiar face. Lyle appears tired, as if he's done this routine a thousand times before. And he has. I know this. Despite what I can't remember, I remember him.

He's still alive? I think to myself.

I watch him as we pass. He's like a ghost. Some apparition that shouldn't be there. A smudge on the window that doesn't belong. The last time I saw Lyle I must have been a teenager. God, how long has it been? How old is this man? He must be nearing eighty.

I catch a hint of a smile on Officer Smith's face. He's fond of the diner; I can tell. The tension I saw on him before appears to melt away. He relaxes in his seat, at ease.

Through the window, Lyle makes eye contact with Officer Smith. His face is stern, wary, a glass being polished in his busy hands. Do they know each other? More than likely. Silvers Hollow has a small police force, something it hardly needs to begin with. I don't doubt that every person here knows everyone else's names.

Officer Smith's smile fades as quickly as it came. My escort saw something reassuring in the Nighthawk Diner, but what? It's pretty much the most beloved landmark in town. I think it would be more unnerving if he *didn't* like it. Suddenly I'm trying to place him. This man, who I've spent miles with in a dark car, hardly five sentences spoken between us. Was he raised here too? I don't recall ever seeing him when I was younger. He's a new face, yet everything about him is familiar.

I feel stupid. It wasn't Lyle that made Officer Smith relax. An older man is sitting in the corner booth near the jukebox. Silky grayish hair, light eyes. The man has excellent posture. His presence is thick with authority and I perceive he's of a military background. He's focused on something in front of him, writing. The man regards Officer Smith through the window, then turns his attention back to the papers on the table in front of him. The stranger doesn't look familiar either. He's alone. I imagine him thinking about his wife, their kids, his grandkids, his shortcomings as a husband or father. My mind runs wild with ideas. This is what I do. Not having much social interaction growing up, I developed a great imagination. I'd watch people out the upstairs bedroom window with Ivy and we'd make up stories about them, who they were. I saw a film called *The Rear Window* when I was much older and realized that it wasn't far off from what our day-to-day lives looked like. As lackluster as that might sound, as children we found it rather thrilling.

Unfortunately, this doesn't sit well with Officer Smith. For some reason he's irritated that I'm staring at the man. The car rolls to a stop and he turns to me. "What's the matter with you?" he asks. "It's not polite to stare."

He's stopped in the middle of the street. I awkwardly glance behind us, expecting to see traffic. A reflexive response, I suppose. There isn't any, obviously. I would say of course there isn't, of course there's no one on the streets at this hour, except that I don't know what "hour" this is. It could be five o'clock in the morning for all I know. Or nine in the evening. The Nighthawk Diner is open twenty-four hours a day. Always has been. Always will be.

Officer Smith twists his head a bit more to face me. The act looks painful for him. I hear a brittle crack in his neck. The sound reminds me of a mummy coming to life after centuries in a sarcophagus. He winces with some measure of pleasure or pain. I can't tell which his expression conveys more accurately. He's in his fifties, but his bones tell me he's closer to a hundred.

The silence in the car is unbearable.

"Are you sure you're all right?" he asks me.

As he waits for a response, I can't tell if he's genuinely concerned, or just plain annoyed.

I want to tell him that something is wrong, but I can't. He'd never understand. No person would. Even if I were having this conversation with a clone of myself, I would probably laugh, chalk it up as absurd.

He waits patiently for me to answer, the car stopped in the middle of Main Street, trapped in the emerald glow of the Nighthawk Diner.

"Nothing," I say with a sigh. "Nothing at all."

Next stop: Tom's Pharmacy. Apparently.

Even though the entire town is less than a couple square miles, it has taken us close to an hour to arrive here.

At the pharmacy.

We're still in the town plaza. He's somehow managed to stretch this drive into an hour-long affair. At this rate, I foresee a long night ahead of me.

The conversation with Officer Smith back at the depot, was...well, *weird*. Then we went to the river, and things took a turn into outright bizarre.

This entire trip has been like a dream. One vivid,

bizarre fever dream. I'm tempted to call it a nightmare, but nothing necessarily bad has transpired. Aside from whatever happened to the back of my head, I mean.

The itch is back. There's something under my skin. I can feel it. As I wait, I chew at the ends of my nails, then use the jagged tips to grate my forearm.

Then there's smoke. Like the scent of burning diesel and oil. The fumes are in my sinuses and it sticks to my clothes and skin. I think that maybe the car is on fire, so I lean forward to find nothing out of the ordinary.

Maybe this cut on my head is worse than I thought...

I reach up and touch the back of my skull again. I expect to wince when my fingers make contact, but not this time. It doesn't hurt anymore. No throb. No ache. No pain. Nothing. The blood has dried. I do a double take at my fingers, unconvinced. I think maybe it's the poor lighting, so I hold them closer to the car window. The light from the pharmacy's sign illuminates my fingertips. The stains are gone.

We're parked at an angle in front of the pharmacy. The parking meters trail up and down the sidewalk.

Parking meters. Still. And these aren't the fancy digital ones that take VISA cards. These run on change, just as they always have. I can't fathom how it still exists in a different time than the rest of the world.

Maybe that's why I left. Because I didn't want to stay the same. I wanted to change. I wanted to grow. To move forward, away from my past. Silvers Hollow is anything but change. It's the thought of progress entombed in ice, frozen in a perpetual stasis in the form of a small, New England town. I can't begrudge the townsfolk for falling in love with its charm. It is tempting, ordinarily. Seductive, even. A place that exists at the end of the rainbow under the warm rays of the sun. But that life isn't for me. It never was.

What's taking so long? I wonder. Officer Smith has been gone for nearly ten minutes. Out the window, I can see shelves of orange pill bottles through the glass door. The ones with the little white caps. There are two antique bells hanging from a ribbon tied to the handle.

Whatever time it is, it's still open. It must be earlier than I thought.

Officer Smith told me he needed to stop here and run

in to get something. I can't imagine what. I don't even know where he's taking me, stretching out a normal twenty-minute drive into an all-night affair. The police station isn't in the cards. We passed it a while ago, after our excursion into the woods. I don't know whether I'm under his protection or under arrest.

I twist in the seat and look out the back window. We're the only car in the entire town plaza except one. A red Mustang. It's parked a couple spaces down from us in front of Hallowed Grounds. There's no one inside the car or the coffee shop. The interior is lit up, but I can't see any patrons. It reminds me of one I used to see on the next street over from where we lived.

Where is everyone?

I rub my eyes. I'm tired. Exhausted even. It's too late at night for this detour into the *Twilight Zone*. At least I think it is.

Goddamn it, where is my watch?

An insidious mist creeps out from the side streets and alleys. Smoky wisps in the shape of tentacles curl around light posts and columns. They engulf the gazebo. Gone are the laughing families and their golden retrievers and the children's dazzling kites.

If there was a kite here, right now, it would be red. I know it.

High above the fog, the endless round bulbs frame the rooftops. I admire it for a moment. The dim, amber spheres are as lovely as I remember them. And yet I can't help but see something else when I look at them. Like a mask on something ugly to hide what it really is.

The more time I've spent in this car, the longer my eyes have had time to focus. The black paneling pulls itself together. The curves settle into straight lines. The hazy contours sharpen.

The car, it's...old?

I study the interior a moment more. His computer, the mirrors, the dash, even the fabric used for the seats. This car is older. *Much* older than it rightfully should be. There's nothing modern about it. The computer is dated. No hi-tech gadgetry, no radio. Now that I think about it, his shoulder radio is missing as well. Don't police always have those nowadays?

I need a better look. I scoot forward on the bench seat and lace my fingers through the metal grating. The metal is ice. I can't help but feel like a frightened animal back here.

He's left the keys. I see them swaying from the ignition along with an Elvis keychain. At least he has good taste in music. The plastic is yellowed, as if it's been sitting out in the sun for twenty years. That doesn't seem like a very smart move on his part. What if I wanted to steal his car? Just start it up and drive away in the middle of the night. Never to be seen again. This is one of the most trusting policemen I've ever met.

It's then that I realize there *is* no computer. There never was. This car is much too old to have one. The other fixings are there. The steering column consists of two ebony rings with a blue circle in the middle. Vintage workings of a vintage car. A long shotgun stands erect in the center of the console, fastened by a locked bracket. Even the weapon seems out of place, the stock fashioned from a wood you hardly see today.

Everything is here, more or less. But not the computer.

Instead, there's a foil-green giftwrapped box. It's puzzling to see. How is it possible that I mistook this for a computer screen? The surface must have refracted the light. I didn't see a glowing screen at all; I saw a shiny gift. The presence of this oddity supersedes the unexplained relic I'm sitting in.

I have to remind myself to breathe.

I can't take my eyes off the box. It's mesmerizing. The perfect creases. The unblemished surface. The shamrock foil wrapping paper. And the black ribbon tied into a perfect bow on top. I see an illogical beauty in this tiny, perfect box. The color shimmers with life, greeting me. I smile a little.

Pandora's Box. A silly thought, but somehow it doesn't seem so silly on this night.

And the worst part is, my first impulse is to grab it, this secret, which has manifested into physical form. To tear it open and peek inside to see what waits for me.

Did I mention that my favorite color is green?

He's left me sitting here, in the back of the car, for *twenty-five minutes*. No explanation. No warning. Nothing. He strikes me as inconsiderate.

It's still there, the box. It's obnoxiously shiny. It glimmers with a clandestine sheen. There's no tag on it. No card. Only the perfectly wrapped black bow. Before this night is through, I'm going to find out what's inside that perfect little box. It's become an obsession. Don't ask me why. I couldn't tell you. So many things have led me here. I just don't know what any of them are. A lot of people don't believe in fate, but I do.

I look in through the window of the pharmacy. One row after another of those amber-colored pill bottles. There must be thousands of them. Are so many people medicated in a town of less than a thousand? What is he doing here? It's driving me nuts, all this waiting.

To my surprise, he left the car doors unlocked again. You'd think he'd have learned his lesson after the first time.

Before I know it, I'm out of the car. I go to open the front passenger door but hesitate. I'm worried he'll catch me. Not only would I be escaping, but now I'd be stealing, too. A rogue shard of light bounces off the box, bringing a green sparkle to my eyes.

The pharmacy door opens.

Officer Smith is standing there, a coffee in each hand, confusion swimming on his face.

"What are you doing?" he asks.

He's not quite as old as I initially thought. He's freshly-shaven; there's a thick mustache over his upper lip. It's pronounced, much more so than his thin eyebrows. I study his face. He's handsome in a way, but nothing special. He's well-groomed. His sideburns are neatly trimmed, his eyes alert. His face is softer than I'd expect of a man of the law.

But his eyebrows... There's something strange about them. They're almost...*feminine*. Like he plucks them. They don't match his mustache. One's thick, the other much thinner. The color even seems slightly different. Am I imagining this?

His eyes narrow while mine grow wider.

"Like I told you before, it isn't polite to stare," he says. He steps out, letting the door swing closed behind him. The air whooshes by the wall of glass, forced back inside the pharmacy.

He's still holding the two cups in his hands. I can see the wisps of heat coming from the lids. It reminds me of seeing the blacktop in summer, how the heat ripples the air, interrupts it.

"Here," he says, holding a coffee out in front of him.

I regard him suspiciously.

"It's coffee," he says. "You look like you could use it."

Coffee. He stopped at the pharmacy and left me outside in the car for twenty-five minutes to get coffee?

This is an estimate, of course. I wouldn't know since I have no watch. What's even more odd about this, is that Hallowed Grounds is right down the street. *Literally* thirty feet. And anyone that lives in Silvers Hollow knows they have the best coffee in town. Maybe the world. Why he's chosen to get coffee from "Tom's Pharmacy" is beyond me.

He catches me looking toward Hallowed Grounds.

"A simple thank you will suffice," he says, pushing the coffee into my hands.

I take the Styrofoam cup from him. It's warm, but definitely not hot. He must have poured it a while ago. The heat feels good against my palms. I like the way the Styrofoam feels. Soft. Warm. I squeeze my fingers into the spongy surface, making barely detectable indentations. It forms to my hand, perfectly fitting my cold fingers.

Officer Smith walks to the car, setting his coffee on the roof while he attempts to fish the keys out of his pocket.

"They're in the car." My voice is blunt and he looks up and a moment passes between us as though he knows I could have escaped or stolen his car and didn't.

He smiles, and there's a warmth there, the same

temperature as the coffee and he meets my eyes and says, "Thank you."

Ah, the car. Now I have a full view of it. It's a lot bigger than I'd have thought. I didn't pay much attention to it before. After all, nobody really looks that closely at a police car when they're arrested.

Old wouldn't begin to describe Officer Smith's wheels. It's round, like a car from the 50s, and brings to mind Tommy guns and Rockabilly. It's built like a tank. There's a single red dome light on top. A "cherry," so to speak. I wonder how bright it is when it's turned on. It could probably light up the entire town plaza with a red strobe, transform it into a Martian wasteland. While I haven't been home in as long as I can remember, I know Silvers Hollow surely must be using modern interceptors by now.

Father would love this car. He was a self-proclaimed 1950s fanatic. He told us on more than one occasion that he wished he could go back and live there forever, back when things were simpler. Before the world decayed and turned into a place he didn't recognize.

Unable to hold it in, a sharp chuckle escapes me. Officer Smith looks up.

"What's so funny?" he asks.

"I don't know." I raise my cup, motioning toward the car. "What's with the car?"

His brow pulls together by invisible strings. It's as though he has no idea his car is decades old. "What do you mean? What's wrong with it?"

"I mean, why are you driving *this*? It looks like it's sixty years old."

"You're acting like you've never seen a police car before."

"Oh, I have. Just never one this...ancient?"

"*Ancient?*"

"Yes."

He snatches the cup from the roof and looks at me with the same miserable eyes I saw before. There's something in them that's pitying, compassionate. He feels bad for me for some reason. He smiles sadly, turning away.

"Are you *sure* you're feeling all right?" he asks.

"Of course I am. I already told you that. Why?"

He lets out a heavy, troubled breath as he looks at me. "Come on, let's get you home."

I can't tell what time it is when I wake. My world has become "timeless," literally. There are no clocks that I've seen. No watches, no clocks hanging on the walls, none even in the one car I've ridden in. I can't even get a vague idea from the sun, because I've yet to see it. It's as if time has never existed at all.

The linens draping the windows are dark. It's still night out. I have no recollection of falling asleep or even getting home, for that matter.

I'm in bed. *My* bed. In my childhood home in Silvers Hollow. My parents live at 17 Haunter Drive. It sounds sinister, but it's really not. If anything, it's the idyllic suburban cul-de-sac. The American Dream.

My parents are fairly normal in some ways, but not so much in others. I always thought of them as conventional, but people can't so easily be put into little boxes now, can they? "Normal" is a relative term. My normal wouldn't be the equivalent as someone say, living in Cape Town's normal. My parents live in a two-story, middleclass home. It's reminiscent of the early Colonial styles, complete with the side-gabled roof, decorative white molding and perfectly symmetrical windows.

The neighborhood is quiet. I think that's what they love most about living here. People pretty much keep to themselves. They wave on Sunday mornings when they mow their perfect green lawns or say hi when they stroll out to get the morning paper. It's calm, peaceful. Some might even say serene. As good a place as any to start a family and settle down.

If you can afford it.

Because with all of that perfection comes a price—one that most middleclass families can't afford. I'd be lying if I said that didn't breed resentment. I never had to worry about that, though. Mother and Father have always been wealthy, even before Ivy or I were born. The majority of the people on this street are. It's how they afford to stay here.

I throw off the covers and swing my legs off the bed. I feel the soft carpet between my toes. It's shaggy. I like the way it tickles my skin.

The throb from the back of my head is nonexistent now, replaced with one in my temples. My guess would be dehydration. My throat feels horrid, dry and dusty. I need something to drink.

How long have I been sleeping for?

Officer Smith must have brought me home.

Momentarily, I relax just a smidge. Being back in this house has allowed my heightened worry to ease.

The room is dark. I can see a faint light beyond the drapes coming from the lampposts that dot the street. No moonlight, though, only the artificial amber radiating from the charming lampposts.

This is by far the darkest night I've ever experienced in this town. It's as if the moon doesn't exist at all. I don't remember seeing any stars, either. I miss lying in my hammock in the backyard, watching them twinkle. Ivy and I used to look for hours here when we were kids. Feeling so small in a world we could get lost in.

Good memories. These are the first to come back.

But I can't think about that now. I have to focus. Be in the now, here, in my bedroom. In my childhood home in Silvers Hollow.

I hear a light tapping on the wood in the hallway and look up to find Bob, our black Labrador Retriever, in the entrance to the bedroom. His nails make that sound when he waddles on the hardwood. His name started out as a joke between Ivy and I, but somehow ended up sticking. Now I can't imagine it as anything else. His coarse hair is medium-length, and there's a patch of white running along his chest. I've run my hands through that fur a million times.

I smile.

Bob tilts his head to the side, panting. I go to hold out my hand and he flinches, taking a step back.

"What's the matter, boy, don't you recognize me?" I

ask. "Bob? It's me."

Bob just stares at me with his big, glassy eyes. I must have changed quite a bit from the last time he saw me, I think. Shot up a few inches since then. I go to take a step forward but he runs away before I can reach him. Does he not recognize me?

I flip the light switch on, recoiling from the flash and pulling my eyes closed. The light is jarring, almost paralyzing. It's too bright. Too white. I go to turn it off, but before my fingers can flip the switch, I see my new bedroom.

It's the same layout. There's a bed, a desk, a closet, and a full-length mirror. All the same pieces of the furniture puzzle are there, but they're different now. Someone has rearranged them.

The color scheme has changed. The comforter that I loved so much is gone, replaced with one I don't care for. The colorful wallpaper I hold fondly in memories has been removed, refurnished with a golden, hexagonal pattern. It's cold. Unwelcoming.

My skin crawls, and I cross my arms. There's no wind

outside, but in here, there's a chill. They say that when a ghost is near you, the air drops in temperature. That's how I feel now. Like a ghost is standing right behind me, as absolutely close as it can be without touching me. Gooseflesh tears across my skin like wildfire and the hairs stiffen.

I stare at the bold pattern on the walls. It moves, like an optical illusion. Something is off about this room. The new wallpaper is disorienting; I can't look at it too long because it brings a heavy ache to my eyes.

Silvers Hollow has changed, if only through subtle, easy-to-miss differences. Or is it me that's changed?

The only thing worse than seeing all these barely perceivable differences is that I can't actually remember if they *are* different. They say memory is one of the most inaccurate things in the world, and that what we can't recall, we fill in using fragments from other broken recollections. Is that the case right now? Am I just remembering wrong? Was my room like this the whole time, and I only think it wasn't? Was that sign on the way into town really red all along, and I only thought it was blue?

I slink to the desk. There's a framed black and white photograph. This is where I kept it—our only complete family portrait. The silver frame gleams, channeling my attention to the picture. It should be empty. I know it should be empty. After all, the photo is tucked safely in my back pocket.

No...

I fumble with my pant pocket, jerking the picture from it so carelessly it almost rips.

It's the same.

The exact same photograph.

Mother. Father. Ivy. Me. The same photograph, the same smiles, the same church. All taken on the same day. I hold the snap out in front of me, comparing it to the doppelganger in the frame. There's no disputing it. It's identical.

"It can't be..." I whisper.

I violently seize the frame, bringing it before my eyes.

No. Just—no. This is impossible. How can there be a copy of this photograph whilst the real one is in my very hands? The polaroid didn't come from some roll of negatives; it wasn't taken by one of those disposable cameras you can buy at the corner drugstore or Tom's Pharmacy. It's a one-of-a-kind picture. Irreplaceable.

An urge comes over me. Whether from sheer fright or confusion or rage I cannot say. I impale the glass on the corner of the desk. The glass shattering is mortifyingly loud in the silent house. It shrieks down the hallway like a banshee.

Bob begins to bark. He's scared. So am I.

I pry the photograph from the mat and hold them both before my eyes. They're the same. Even the weathering matches. The creases, the dirt. Everything. I don't understand what's happening. What is going on?

I'm panicked. I'm hyperventilating. I'm shaken. I hold a hand to my chest, reminding myself to breathe.

My eyes bounce back and forth between the pictures, pleading to find something—anything, that's different.

Just as I'm about to give up, I suck in a deep breath and flip them over.

There.

I don't know how I missed it before. It was right there—right in front of my face the whole time.

Written across the back of the original photograph are four simple, scribbled words. They look like they were written quickly. Rushed. Urgent. I trace them with my eyes over and over, letting the copy fall away to the floor.

I shudder, a menacing fear taking hold of me.

My mind reels. This must be a joke. Someone is playing a joke on me. A cruel, heartless joke. I look up. My eyes dart around the room, half expecting to find a hidden camera crew filming my reaction for the entire world to see.

But no. There's no one. I'm alone in this bizarre amalgamation of my childhood bedroom and a nightmare holding a photograph I haven't seen in twenty years. And what it has written on the back sends a shiver to my heart.

it's All a Lie

I'm speeding down the rabbit hole. I see spirals of blood and vivid, swirling green eyes leering at me nestled in hollow trees and the frigid air turns my skin to ice while the echo of voices carries on around me. I hear bats flap and screech all around me and I keep picking up speed and rocket from the life I know to the life I left behind. The feeling is inescapable, and crushing.

And when I finally open my eyes, I'm in a deeper level of the dream world. A place where my memories hide around every corner like spectral beasts. Where every safe place and comforting thought is desecrated and ruined.

It's all a lie.

Those seemingly small but incredibly potent words have shattered this fish-bowl world.

I can't breathe.

The photographs quiver as my hands tremble, and in the street beyond the window I see a woman looking up at me from the shadows. She's an apparition. A blur. That's what I'm seeing, yes. I move closer to the window, and gasp. My heart catches in my throat.

I rush forward. The streetlight flickers down below. She's gone. And I wonder, was she ever really there?

The house is quiet. *Too* quiet. The kind of quiet where you can hear a pin drop, or someone breathing behind you. The tick of a watch. So many dreadful things.

I make my way to my parents' room, expecting to find them asleep in bed.

They're not.

Their room is as empty as the rest of this town. It's shrouded in shadows, deserted. The bed is made, no creases in the comforter or dents in the pillows. Nothing is out of place. Not that I would know. Ivy and I rarely came in here. It was off-limits. This isn't so different, I tell myself.

With the exception of Ivy, I was alone in the house a lot of the time when I was a child while my parents worked. In that aspect, it very much still feels like home right now.

Every time I turn a corner in this sprawling house I find Bob waiting for me, studying my every move from the opposite end of the hall. He's curious. Guarded. We watch each other in the sullen light of the hallway. It's as if we've never known each other at all. Like I've never ran my fingers through his fur, scratched his big, droopy ears, or fallen asleep with his head on my chest. He used to follow me everywhere I went when I was a kid. Everywhere.

Now all he sees is an intruder. An intruder in my own home. Imagine that. He needs time, that's all. He'll come around.

He's silent, sitting there looking all Bob-like. An unkempt mass of black fur with a white patch on his chest. His eyes are impossible to see in here. I know that if I could see them, they'd be suspicious of me. I begin to move toward him and he scampers down the stairs. I check the doors upstairs, making my way down the hall. I peek into each of the rooms, and all I can think about is what's written on the back of that photograph. *It's all a lie.* The words send a shock to my bones. I clench my jaw. A myriad of questions pop up in my mind like a fleet of rusted buoys. Dreamy white letters floating across an abyss of nothingness.

Who wrote it?

What does it mean?

What are they trying to tell me?

But most importantly: Where is everybody?

Even though Officer Smith wasn't the warmest person I've ever encountered, his company beat being alone. Come to think of it, he's the only person I've seen aside from that man in Nighthawk's. And Lyle, of course.

I'm so thirsty. My throat is bone-dry. My lips are cracked. I run my tongue across them, and when I try to force a smile I feel them pull apart painfully. I sweep my tongue across them again and taste blood. I run my fingertip along my bottom lip and find it speckled with bright blood.

Downstairs, Bob is sitting in the middle of the living room watching me. The safety I'd normally feel with him around is nonexistent. He's changed since I've been gone. He used to be my protector. Today he's a friend I don't recognize.

"Are you just going to sit there and stare at me all night?" I ask. "Bob? I know you can hear me." He knows what I'm saying. He might be a dog, but he understands. He's always been smarter than other dogs. Once we even saw him stand on his hind legs and open my bedroom door. It was funny at the time, but when I think about it now, it just seems…creepy. I don't know what I would do if I saw him open a door right now. In the right context something can seem comical, but in the wrong one, unbelievably frightening.

Bob tilts his head. The luminosity from the window paints him in a light fitting akin to Picasso's "Blue Period." I can see his eyes now. They look like a slick of oil, wet and dark.

"Well. All right then."

I try and ignore him while he sits there watching me. I inspect the room. They've redecorated since I've been home. My parents usually stick with muted colors, but not now. I used to think it was pretentious, but now I realize that it was merely because it was easier to decorate. In the house's current state, they seem to have taken a liking to more vibrant tones.

Reds, more specifically. Although there are undertones with oranges, and golds. I don't care for it much; it's uninviting. It doesn't feel like home. Even though these colors are technically warm on the color spectrum, they're somehow cold in here. Invasive. Forced. They've violated all of my memories with this bizarre color scheme. I don't know why. It's unlike them. The furniture is equally strange. They've swapped out the couch and chairs for retro pieces. It looks like they copied a page out of an IKEA catalog from sixty years ago.

I peer toward the hall and see the door to the cellar.

A shiver runs through me.

I'd forgotten this door; consciously *tried* to forget it. This was the only door in the house I was never allowed to open. My parents weren't fond of me going in their bedroom, but the cellar, well, that was absolutely restricted.

The cellar door was painted red, and it still is now.

Not just ordinary fire engine red, but a dark red, the color of a ruby. My parents never did explain why I wasn't allowed down there, even as I'd grown older. And during our entire childhood together, that door was somehow the only source of conflict between Ivy and myself, the only reason we ever fought. Thankfully, it rarely came up.

You see, Ivy *was* allowed in the basement. She would go with Father, usually in the evenings. He'd never really call her to go with him; she just went when he went. Usually at the same time on the same days. It was routine. They'd be gone for hours and hours, until finally Ivy would creep back to bed at practically midnight. Sometimes she had tears in her eyes. This started when she was maybe five or six, and didn't stop until the day she moved out. Neither of them would talk about what went on down there, and I never asked Ivy about it. I figured she'd talk when she was ready to. I once tried to ask Father what was in the basement, but he just smiled at me, almost sad like, and went back to his book.

And now, standing here, this is my chance.

I tiptoe through the moonlight until I'm right in front

of that big red door. I feel tiny in front of it, just like I did when I was younger. I feel like if I touch it, it'll awaken from its slumber, a sleeping giant.

The doorknob is cold against my fingertips, like touching the surface of a snowball.

My breath snags; my pulse begins to race.

As my fingers tighten around the handle, I close my eyes and take a deep breath.

I stand there in front of the door, my fingers wrapped around the handle, and no matter what I tell myself, I can't work up the courage to pull it open and see what's on the other side.

I listen to my heartbeat in my ears, rising like an alarm.

I rip my hand away from the door like it's red-hot metal.

I can't. Not today. Not now. Not ever.

A girl is crying. She's weeping softly, the way a child would, and I slowly stir from my slumber. The sound is close. It resonates as if I'm in a cave, deep underground.

Immediately, I know it's Ivy. Oh, God, my mind shrieks. What's happened? Her cries send me spiraling face first into a well of panic. But I can't find her anywhere, only listen helplessly as she whimpers and moans.

"Ivy?" My voice comes out like dust, like my lungs are filled with sand. I don't recognize it.

I'm surrounded by darkness. The heat in the room is stifling. I can't breathe. I struggle to sit up, fighting the bed.

My feet become tangled as I extricate myself from the blankets, and I crash to the floor with a heavy thud.

Ivy sobs louder, and I know she's in pain, and I'm moving as quickly as I can to get to her. I see nothing but her silhouette against a sliver of light. She's standing just beyond my bedroom door, eclipsed in the dim hall light.

"Ivy, I'm here."

I fumble in the darkness, knocking over the items on my bookcase before reaching the light switch.

She begins to wail louder yet, and it's protracted and horrible, as if someone is hurting her.

Dread seizes me in place, and my hand fumbles until I find the switch on the wall.

I flip it.

The light blooms just as I glimpse Ivy beyond the door. She's looking down at her gown in shock, her hands raised slightly as though they're not her own. There's deep, dark bruises spotting her pale arms and the breath is knocked out of me.

I want to scream, to beg for someone to save us, for anyone to hear our cries for help, but I can't. I only make pathetic whimpering noises. I want to help her so badly because I'm her big sister and she needs me.

Ivy tries to speak but nothing comes out because she's too panicked to form words and I hear a scream begin to climb in her throat.

I turn to stone, my face twisted in horror and utter agony, and I see terror flare in Ivy's helpless eyes as she realizes that her gown is covered in blood. And then, she screams.

I need a drink.

I pull open the refrigerator door to find half-empty shelves. There's a pitcher of water with chunks of ice floating on the surface. It looks invigorating, refreshing. It reminds me of Antarctica. I hold the pitcher up and guzzle down as much water as I can stomach. The cold feels amazing against my dry lips; it soothes the cracks in my skin and washes away the scabs of blood. Dribbles of chilled water leak from my lips as I drink, like I'm a survivor who just emerged from the wilderness after being lost for months on end.

On the verge of a brain freeze, I set the pitcher back

on the shelf and wipe my mouth with the back of my hand. The frosty water spills through my organs like roaring white rapids, waking me up.

An IV of cold filters through my blood and suddenly I'm submerged in a reverie.

Billowing smoke. Fire. I see visions of a violent, unnatural storm. Bodies fastened to the horizon instead of stars. But most of all, there is death. I hear the hollow echo of thunder and a burning red sky.

A guilt I can't fathom permeates from my moist skin and I hear that heavy, whirling sound rising.

Then, just like that, I'm back in the kitchen. I fight the compulsion to vomit everything up into the sink, and I stand there, hands on the counter, letting the grisly feeling pass.

I shakily move back to the fridge. There's a few sodas and condiments, but nothing of any real sustenance. I reach in and take out a glass bottle of Coca-Cola. I haven't seen one of these in ages. They still sell them of course, but I don't know many people who still buy the kind in the glass bottles. They taste better, the glass-bottled sodas.

There's just something about them that I love. They feel more *grand*. More real. A little bit of magic in a bottle.

I look more closely inside the fridge and see that there's 7up, too. Also in those recognizable glass bottles. When did Mother and Father start buying these things? I shove the bottle back inside and close the door as if there's a flying rodent inside. I brace myself, resting my head on the door.

I open my eyes to find a bone-colored business card glaring at me from the front of the refrigerator door. My eyes twitch, then widen. The rectangle glows against the door, like the moon against the night sky that I remember before this town.

I remove the magnet, taking the card in my hands. It feels weighty, expensive. It has raised lettering, the typeface a gold foil rather than a stark black. Clever. The metallic letters compliment the subtle off-white cardstock but stand out just enough to be visible. Much I presume, like a good therapist would hope to be in a patient's life. An influence rather than a direct thought.

Doctor Aurora Snow, Clinical Psychologist. I've never

heard this name before. It doesn't even sound remotely familiar. Pretty, though. It rolls off the tongue. Handwritten on the bottom is a note in elegant cursive that says:

Don't forget appointment Friday

There's no time written down. Or a date. I flip it over expecting to find another note, but there's nothing. Did I write this? Or did she? There's an address on the bottom buried beneath the cursive. I know this place. It's on Main Street, not far from Tom's Pharmacy and Hallowed Grounds and everything else in Silvers Hollow. Only a stone's throw away.

I turn around, the card in hand, to face Bob, as though he could tell me what this is. It's an absurd thought. He's still waiting patiently, looking up at me with those big black eyes. His nose is wet. He opens his mouth, panting. His floppy tongue hangs from the side of his mouth. He's waiting for me to solve the mystery I hold in my hand.

I look around the room for some kind of note— anything that might point me to where my parents have disappeared to. But there's nothing here.

Is this even still our house? Maybe to them. Not to me. They've changed so much it's almost unrecognizable. Even Bob is acting funny for God's sake. He probably can't stand it either.

Have my parents been seeing a therapist? I haven't spoken to them for months now. The last time I talked to my Father, we'd had a falling out. I think they knew it was a long time coming. We've always had problems.

Did I cause this? Create a rift between them when I left? I should call them. Then I'll know they're okay. They're probably just out to dinner or a movie or on vacation. Or at their *new* home in the city, the one they spend most of their time at nowadays.

I need to call someone. Anyone.

Where's the phone? It's missing from the wall beside the refrigerator.

A shrill ringing explodes. It's so loud I feel like it's rattling my bones.

There it is. They moved it. The phone has been relocated to the wall across from the fridge.

It keeps ringing, the receiver rattling the entire wall.

Wait a minute…

It's…a *rotary phone*? What the hell? Why is there a rotary phone in here?

The handset shakes against the base, almost louder than before. Its wail is unbearable.

I can't take it anymore. I pick it up.

It's an automated recording of a cheery female voice.

"Hello! Please arrive at least ten minutes early for your scheduled appointment time."

For my appointment? My parents' appointment?

"Due to the emergency, there are limited availabilities and cancellation fees will apply."

My voice cracks the silence. "What emergency?"

To my shock, the automated voice responds. "Why, the Event, of course."

I do a double take. My eyes pull together. So it *isn't* a recording. It's a live person who happens to *sound* like a recording. "Oh, I'm sorry," I find myself apologizing, "I thought you were—"

"No apologies necessary," the voice says. It's polite, cheery. I imagine the receptionist on the other end of the phone smiling as she talks. "If you wish to reschedule, please call us back at your earliest convenience."

"Wait," I say, my fingers tightening around the receiver. Finally, some vague evidence of the time. It's Friday?

"Yes?" the voice asks, infinitely patient.

"Appointment for whom?"

Silence. There's a long pause between us. Something seems off about this call. I can't put my finger on what. This doesn't feel right.

I muster the courage to speak. "For my parents?" Stupid. She doesn't know who I am much less who my parents are.

"No."

"Ivy, then?"

"No, ma'am." The receptionist's tone drops an octave.

Who calls at night to confirm a doctor's appointment? Especially for one scheduled the same day?

"Then who?"

"Why, for you, of course."

My heart sinks. My hands begin to tremble. The

phone turns to a bar of lead in my hand.

"What?" My voice barely comes out. "No, there must be some mistake, I've never seen—"

"I'm afraid not, ma'am. You scheduled it yourself last week after your appointment with Dr. Snow. I spoke to you myself."

I try to say something but my words are choked off. I can't speak.

"Have a nice day!"

Then, a dial tone.

I'm standing in the driveway, baffled by what I've heard. It's still night. I've been standing here, beside the exceedingly green grass, for nearly ten minutes. I've become a statue in front of our house. Like a lawn gnome. Or those rickety metal flowers. I feel paralyzed, and I ooze with anxiety. People might even be a little frightened if they saw me. Fortunately, I don't have to worry about that because there's no one around. Our little corner of the world is deserted.

I can't see any stars. The overcast must be blotting them out still. It's humid here. The air, it's sticky. Wet. Stuffy, and uncomfortable. Why can't there be a breeze?

PATRICK DELANEY

Where has the wind gone? I miss the coast. The Redwoods and the sea and the brine. The openness.

Crickets. It sounds like dozens of them. They chirp from the darkness, serenading each other from everywhere and nowhere. The ominous silence of Silvers Hollow makes their tiny melodic voices magnified, much louder than they really are. That, interspersed with the humidity, makes me feel like I'm in the middle of a bayou. It's sorta nice to hear them after the quiet that I've been immersed in since the train depot. It makes me feel not quite so alone.

My parents are gone. This much I know. I checked every room in the house and turned up nothing but webs and dust. It's as though nobody has lived in this house at all. Like they got up and left it behind to rot. For their other, grander home.

Only that picture was there, which tells me they must still live here. The house *is* filled with things. Clothes and knickknacks and appliances. Just not the things I recognize. It feels more like a hotel. Impersonal. Forgettable. Artificial.

I wander through the chill in the air to the sidewalk,

casting a glance toward town. Around the bend, I can see the same glow of all those twinkling bulbs.

Our neighborhood is connected to town like an artery feeding the heart. Haunter Lane bisects Maple Street and feeds straight into the town plaza. I can practically see the church from our front yard. The proximity made it a short walk to the store for groceries, a cup of coffee at Hallowed Grounds, or even a midnight movie at the Starlight Theater.

I gaze at all of the houses. They're uniform, painted with fresh coats of paint in vivid colors, the trim unblemished. The neighborhood looks like it's full of model homes. They're too new. Too perfect. This isn't how I remember it. I mean, it *is*, but it isn't. The years have been stripped away; the wear gone. It's not lived in. This isn't my neighborhood. This is someone else's memory.

I hear a sound. It's consistent. Moving. I recognize it.

Water. Like the slow current of a stream.

I think about the river from before and my heart bats at my ribs. There *was* something there, wasn't there?

I look toward the end of the cul-de-sac and spot a

woman standing two houses down from me. She's holding a hose in one hand, a cocktail in the other.

I spring forward, cutting down the sidewalk as if she's a mirage. I can't lose her. I need to talk to someone— anyone. I can't bear the thought of being alone here another second. I don't risk blinking, forcing my eyes to stay open even when a cloud of gnats swarm my face.

She's so still that at first I think she's a mannequin, placed in the front yard like they had in those towns built to test atomic bombs. But no, she is indeed real.

My presence startles her as I hurry across the lawn. With a gasp, the hose wavers in her hand, spilling out an awkward stream. She recoils, the drink slushing out the top of the glass. There's a little pink umbrella sticking out of it. The glass has crystallized salt along the rim with chunks of crushed ice inside. I can see smeared red where her lips met with the glass. She drops the hose and puts a hand on her chest as if she's going to faint.

What in God's name is this woman doing watering her lawn at this hour?

"I'm sorry, I didn't mean to scare you," I say.

"No, it's all right, dear. It's fine." She pauses. "I'm fine," she says again. She appears to be reassuring herself. She chuckles a little.

The woman says, "You must think I'm crazy."

Ah, so she *does* realize this isn't normal behavior. "Of course not," I reply.

The woman is easily six feet tall. She's all curves, with a mane of flowing red hair and elaborate diamond earrings dangling from her ears. She wears too much lipstick. I can see some of it caked to the front of her stained teeth. The shade is the color of a raw steak. It makes me nauseous thinking about it. Her eyes are sunken behind dark, plum bags. She reminds me of those women who drink mimosas at nine in the morning and gossip way too much about the love lives of relatives.

She wheezes as she gets her breath back. Suddenly she's looking at me in a different light. As if she knows me. Come to think of it, she looks remotely familiar as well. A lot of the past has faded over the years since I've been gone, but there's a morsel still there. A crumb.

She takes a drawn-out sip of her cocktail while eyeing

me. I listen to her slurp down what's left in the glass.

"It's...*you*," she says, astonished.

I don't say anything. I don't know what to say to her. I can't remember. Why can't I remember?

"I know you," she says, her eyes growing wider, crazed. "You're their daughter, aren't you?"

"I'm sorry, I don't..."

"That *is* you, right?" she repeats. "You live there, in that house?" she asks, nodding her head at the house.

"Do I know you?"

Her drink empty, she begins chewing the ice. It sounds like her teeth are breaking inside of her mouth. I imagine them splitting, the nerves exposed and raw. She smiles, and for just a fraction of a second, that lipstick on her teeth looks like blood.

"I heard all about you, tsk-tsk," she says. "Terrible, terrible things I heard. Jesus, you were there that day—"

"What things?" I ask. "I'm sorry, I don't know what you're talking about."

She sighs, caught in a dream-like trance, like I'm not standing right beside her on the lawn. She slowly waves the empty glass at the lawn. Her movements are almost too controlled—like she's some sort of animatronic rather than a real-life person. Like one of those Halloween decorations you put on your porch to scare kids. "Your parents, they're…"

"What are you doing out here?"

She looks around the nighttime neighborhood, not a soul in sight besides the two of us. "What do you mean?"

"I mean…why are you watering your lawn?"

She laughs sharply. "Why wouldn't I? I wouldn't want my beautiful lawn to dry out and die, now would I?"

"But *now*? It's night."

"I'll tell you why," she says drunkenly, with a hiccup. "Because just like everyone else in this town— present company excluded—I paid to live in this little paradise. And I intend to live the brief time I've got left to the fullest." She picks up the hose and starts watering again, like this is an everyday routine for her. A couple more hiccups gurgle out of her throat, and the hose lazily swings back and forth.

I can't let it go, and I say, "But why now?"

She freezes, turning her head to me. I can practically hear the bones crack in her neck. "Because this is where I'm supposed to be." She smiles, but there's something disturbing about it. It's unnatural; manic. It doesn't feel right, or seem true. "Speaking of which, isn't there somewhere *you're* supposed to be, too?"

Okay, this is too weird. Her behavior is so outlandish it's almost to the point of becoming disturbing.

"What time is it?" I ask.

She doesn't answer, just keeps pouring water over the lawn.

I study the robust woman for a minute, watching her practiced actions. She begins to hum a tune quietly, swaying to it, the hose in one hand, the empty glass in the other.

Then I see it. Something until now I had failed to notice. I shift my feet, feeling the surface beneath my shoes. It's soft. Level. Uniformly symmetrical.

This isn't grass; it's fake. There's nothing real about it. I look down, lifting my feet as if I'm standing on quicksand.

No wonder it's so green.

It's not grass; it's AstroTurf.

The town plaza is quite a bit brighter than the rest of Silvers Hollow. It's the nucleus. Full of light, and color. The tendrils of bulbs stretch into the connecting neighborhoods, threading cheer and wonder. Some look like they're floating up there, high above my head, like ghostly lanterns.

I pass along on the sidewalk, unseen in the night, when I come to a newspaper vending machine.

The blue metal box sits alongside another one that's plastic and red, the kind you find real estate magazines in. Or those stupid booklets with the dogs on the covers that nobody ever really reads. Inside the metal one is the town's monthly newsletter. How many people actually read the newsletter? I have no idea. I know I don't. At least I didn't, back then. Father did. He liked to stay informed. They say knowledge is power. If that really is true, then Mother and Father took that philosophy and ran with it. I would know.

The funny thing is, that even despite that fact, they're more of a haze than anything solid. Like two phantoms. It's sort of like seeing someone in a dream. You can tell who they are, and you have a general idea what they look like, but they're out of focus. A shimmer. Muddled.

Don't get me wrong, I know them. I really do. I know what they look like. I remember clearer than a gleaming crystal glass that my mother never started a book she didn't finish, no matter how much she hated it. I remember that she wore the same perfume every single day of her life. One spray to the wrist, another to the nape of her neck from one of those fancy glass bottles with the pump. I know my father, how he used to stand in the backyard with a brass telescope for hours and watch the stars.

It never occurred to me until later that maybe he did that because he wished he'd been anywhere but here. He was always fascinated with concepts that were beyond any of us. Even Mother. And this is a woman who taught quantum mechanics and solved math puzzles for fun.

It wasn't their fault. I think it's just the way they were built. They solved problems. Devoted themselves to fixing things. They loved challenges, loved to *be* challenged. Their minds only had one speed, and it never, ever, shut off. They could never see what was right in front of them. Kids? A broken water heater? Those weren't challenges. They were trivialities. Banal glitches in the game of life. Their only focus was the bigger picture. The things that nobody thought they *could* fix.

On more than one occasion Ivy and I tried to join Father, out there in the backyard. The look in his eyes told us everything we needed to know. That we weren't welcomed in their lives. That we were more ornamental than anything. Like a pair of earrings, or a shiny new car. Pawns, really, on a grand chess board, used in a game. Their game. Their lives. Our lives. My life.

I suppose I shouldn't complain. If any other kid had seen our life from the outside, they would have done anything to trade parents. Mother and Father never swore at us. Never told us when to brush our teeth, or to go to bed. Some might even say we had it made. But what people don't understand is that all that freedom can be isolating. And in the air of all that freedom was a silence that smothered us day after day.

Especially today.

I'm still standing on the sidewalk in front of the newspaper vending machine. Darkness is my only friend tonight. The only constant.

How long have I been waiting here? The time has gotten away from me. I must be more tired than I thought.

I squat down and look closely at the plastic. There are a few random scratches on the surface, like somebody took the edge of a quarter and hacked at the plastic as if it were a knife. I absentmindedly trace the abrasions with my nail. I glance around, at every corner and every window, but there's no one. I bet the lady watering her lawn is gone, too.

It amazes me these are still around. With all of the advances in today's world, they seem like relics now. Antiques. Leftover artifacts from another time, like you might find buried under a sea of sand.

I look closer at the scratches in the plastic, put my face right up to them. Something about these scratches makes me feel sad. I see a correlation between these markings and my life. The plastic shield is formed with heat and matter. It's brought into the world without anyone actually *asking* if it wants to be here. And finally, it is left out in the darkness, exposed to a million terrible things. I think how someone found it here, maybe by chance, and ruined it thoughtlessly, or perhaps even maliciously.

The only question is; did I help myself get to this point? Was *I* a contributing factor in my own destruction?

Ivy and I used to come down to grab the town newsletter for Father. He'd give us a few extra dollars to do with as we pleased. Ivy and I always split our earnings right down the middle. Father was generous in that way. He was a lot of things, but stingy wasn't one of them. Frugal at times, sure. Careful. But always generous. Mother and he regularly donated to charities. They were adamant about contributing to society. There was a sincerity to them that the outside world adored. Even though I knew they didn't care about Ivy or I the way we wanted, it was comforting to know they cared about *something*.

Most people in this town don't know this, but our family's money is part of the reason this town still exists. You want to know how much, I know. Unfortunately, I don't know the specifics. Mother and Father were very private about their finances. I doubt Ivy knew either. We've always had money. Since I can remember. You'd assume that being affluent granted us some lavish, charmed lifestyle growing up. Like those people you see on The Real Housewives of Whatever. But it wasn't like that with us. My parents were careful. They didn't flaunt their money. They weren't vain. They didn't buy fancy things. Father owned an old Chevy Impala most of my childhood. Mother drove a Toyota Corolla with a broken mirror on the passenger side. The only thing we possessed that was marginally more grand was our house. It was bigger, yes, but not by much.

That's a lot of how childhood is. You spend hours, days, years, wondering. Comparing. Seeing where you fit into the world. But now, standing here looking down at this scratched plastic, I see that we never really did. My parents knew this. It's why they worked so hard to be part of the world. They wanted to be validated, like a parking ticket. Be accepted. Loved.

Just like Ivy and I.

The vending machine costs ten cents for a newspaper. Ten. Cents. This machine must be more outdated than I thought, because where I live now, a newspaper is easily $1.50. I reach into my pocket without a second thought. I fish around and find that I have exactly one dime. It's shiny, just like the rest of Silvers Hollow. It appears newly minted, like a tiny round mirror in the palm of my hand.

When the dime drops into the slot, I hear a satisfying metallic clink of acceptance.

I smile. For the first time since I can remember, life seems slightly more bearable.

I reach inside and grab for the top paper.

As I pull it off the stack, a second, folded newspaper falls from inside and lands on the sidewalk at my feet.

The outside newspaper is unexceptional.

The front page reads, SOVIET FIRE EARTH SATELLITE INTO SPACE!

Toward the bottom, there's a second article.

LONG ISLAND TRAINS CRASH; 75 DEAD.

I look closer at the date.

October 4th, 1957?

But this isn't all I've found. I fold the paper unevenly and set it on top of the vending machine, then reach down and snatch up the second.

The second newspaper is the same as all the others. Only it isn't. It's been intentionally hidden from sight. It reminds me of a snake shedding its skin. I have removed one paper and ended up with another. A more genuine one. What makes it feel more authentic than the other? Is it the fact that it was hidden? As if someone went out of their way to place it inside, *knowing* that I would find it?

At that moment the stillness around me is eerily quiet.

This is the definition of night. Or early morning. I can't tell which. Even though it's freezing, the air is still wrought with humidity.

I feel sweat begin to trickle down my sides. Crystal beads skate down my skin, narrowly touching the fabric of my shirt. I dread the moment they'll make contact.

Suddenly, the powerful springs in the vending machine door activate and the heavy metal swings up and slams closed. The noise is loud enough to shock me from my musings. I startle and fall onto my tailbone right there on the sidewalk. I'm bathed under a funnel of depressed light from the post, like I'm rehearsing a scene for a play. It reminds me of an audition I did once for *Hamlet*.

You see, back when I was struggling to feed myself, I worked part-time as a waitress. When I wasn't serving, I must have gone to hundreds of auditions. Most were dingy, hole-in-the-wall productions run out of shady theaters on back alley streets nobody had ever heard of.

When I'd stood there on the stage, before the panel of silhouettes, there was a spotlight on me just like there is now.

In that instance, I'd auditioned for the role of Ophelia, Hamlet's would-be wife. I didn't get the part, but I always remembered a single line from that play. A favorite of mine, now.

A dream itself is but a shadow.

It stuck with me, that line. It means that when we dream, we see remnants of what we've done. The essence of experience. We dream of shadows. And that's exactly where I am now. A world of shadows.

I'm panting from the scare, a mess on the sidewalk looking up at the vending machine. There's a ring of sweat around my collar, my skin clammy and pale. I see the air coming from my mouth and disappearing into the night. My hand is pressed down on my galloping heart.

It's then that I see it. I couldn't before, not where I was standing. But now, sitting half-dazed on the concrete under this sickly light, I see that the scratches in the glass aren't random at all. At this exact angle, peering up from down here, I see something. There's another message.

WHO ARE YOU?

For some reason, I remember the sparkling green gift

box at this precise moment, and I can't help the sneaking suspicion that whatever is inside that box, will tell me everything I need to know.

I would say that I've traveled back in time, except it's already felt like that since I arrived.

I'm in the Nighthawk Diner. I'm starting to like it here. While the house I grew up in has changed in ways I can't even begin to describe, this diner is more or less exactly the same.

There's a glowing jukebox at the far end of a row of booths lined below a wall-sized, plate-glass window. A long counter. Vinyl stools. Black and white checked flooring. Chrome everything. There's a familiar tune playing, but I can't name it. I know I've heard it on the radio before. The song sounds like it's playing on a record rather than CD. I can hear the faint scratches as the needle carves through the vinyl. I hum to myself as I sit in the center booth.

Maybe I've lost my mind? What else could explain all the weird things I've been seeing?

That's two messages now.

An older man in an apron with a sour face and a paper hat is speaking with another man in a suit at the cash register. The man in the suit wears a frown. The man's companions—another older gentleman and two women are waiting at the door, one of the men holding it open.

"Bernard!" one of the women says impatiently.

Bernard tips his head, then heads for the door.

The man in the apron lets the register slam closed, then walks to the foot of my table with a small pad of paper and a pencil. He nods at the two couples as they disappear through the exit.

I know this face.

It's Lyle, the owner of Nighthawk's.

I feel my body relax just a hair. Seeing even just one familiar face is enough to let the tension slacken.

"What'll it be?" he asks.

Lyle was always like this. I haven't seen the man in decades, but he hasn't changed one bit. He's disagreeable to an extent. People might even say rude. I never held it against him, because people have often said the same about me. He's genuine, doesn't believe in hiding behind masks. I respect that. There's something to be admired there, I think. In a world of fake people, he isn't confused about who he wants to be.

Lyle's eyebrows flatten when I don't respond. He tips his head just a little, the way people do when they're being impatient. He taps the pencil on the pad of paper, and there's this moment where we just look at each other.

It feels like a lifetime passes between us.

"You came," he says finally. "I didn't think you would. In fact, I thought you'd be the last person I'd ever see in this town."

I smile at him, because I don't know what else to do.

His eyes find the window and take in the lifeless town plaza. There's something hopeless about them, as though he can't see anything beyond the diner. As if this is all that's left. A diner at the end of the world.

"I saw you on TV," he says.

I sigh, a crease forms between my brow. I think back to my last performance. I'm suddenly wondering how many people saw my face all over the world. Listened to what I offered. Trusted what I promised. I feel a pang of guilt wedge itself in my heart and then there's that sound again. The sound that I can only describe as a whirl. Like giant fan blades.

My eyes start to follow his gaze, and that's when I see her.

The woman.

She's there. Beyond the gazebo.

She's watching me from the darkness. She's pale and awful and her eyes are two red coals burning in black holes. I imagine them sucking in the light of the world.

"You've grown," he adds, snapping my attention like a match.

"What?" I mutter.

"Don't look much different than you used to, though."

His memory is remarkably better than mine.

Somehow, he has been able to recognize me despite a fifteen-year gap.

I can't find any words.

Lyle tucks the notepad into his pocket and skewers the pencil behind his ear and says, "Don't worry, I remember your order." He winks at me and walks off as the bells on the front door jingle.

That's when I see him. The same man from before that I saw through the window when I first got to town. He's an imposing figure to behold, a walking storm stuffed in an expensive suit with a head of silvery hair. He reminds me of a hunter you'd see on a safari. There's an air about him, a confidence. This man is important. I can tell. His clothes and body language speak volumes, tell a story. And his story says he doesn't belong here. That he's not in his natural habitat. I picture a den of animal heads in his house. Maybe a wall of antique guns. Old black-powder pistols and stuffed zebras.

We make eye contact and I see relief in his eyes. His chiseled, stone face turns to putty. The corner of his mouth begins to hook into a smile when his cellphone starts ringing.

It's the most generic ringtone I've ever heard.

Before he can take another step, the phone is in his hand.

I can't hear what he's saying from so far away, but his eyes never leave me during the entire thirty-second conversation with the mystery caller.

His expression changes as he stares at me. His relief pulls into a frown. It's clear to me that he isn't liking whatever he's being told.

Without saying anything, he abruptly snaps the phone shut and smiles wistfully before walking back out the entrance.

Lyle is back. He sets a plate down in front of me with a simple tuna sandwich, a slice of dill pickle, and a glass of water. I haven't eaten this kind of food since I was a teenager. My palate now is more…refined.

I look up to find him standing there with his hands on his hips. He looks like he hasn't had a customer in years.

"Where is everyone?" The words leave my mouth as if I'm on autopilot.

Lyle exhales, swallowing. He's uncomfortable with the direction of my line of questioning.

"What time is it?" I ask.

Lyle bites his lip thoughtfully.

"This isn't how this works," he says.

"Why aren't there any people—outside?"

Lyle looks at me strangely, as if I've just asked him why the sky is blue, or the grass green. "Why do you *think*?" His tone is a little snarky, even for Lyle.

"Sorry," I say. I lower my eyes to my sandwich and my sad little pickle. "Right, yeah, of course."

Lyle exhales, a shade guilty for snapping at me, then swallows. "Just…try not to worry, all right? I know it's weird being back, but you'll be all right, after a while."

Lyle walks away and I turn and look out at the plaza.

The woman with the black holes for eyes is gone.

A couple comes in by the time I'm finished with half of my tuna sandwich.

They walk right by me like I'm invisible.

The man is older, maybe in his late forties. The woman is easily half his age. I watch them, trying to deduce if she's his daughter or his lover. His hair is dark, hers light. Both are quite tall. Not freakishly tall, but tall enough to stand out from the average man and woman. Their faces are wired into grim expressions, like they've both been handed death sentences and are awaiting execution.

They're in the booth furthest from me, next to the jukebox. The man has his back to me, obscuring the woman's face.

I can hear them talking, hear their muffled voices and subtle movements. They act as though someone is eavesdropping on them, recording their every word. The oddest thing about this, though, is that they're speaking in another language. I think it's German. They don't laugh, or smile. They don't do much of anything except sit and whisper to each other.

I'm not quite sure what to make of them, these two.

When Lyle approaches the couple, they ease back against their respective sides of the booth and finally, *finally*, break into a smile.

Lyle on the other hand, does not smile.

The man quickly becomes agitated. He's speaking English now. His voice climbs until I hear him say, "Eat? How can we possibly eat at a time like this?" He's practically yelling as he says this last part. He's not yelling out of anger, though. He's worried about something. Clearly the same something that's twisted his face into the frown he wore into the diner.

The woman reaches for his hand, attempting to allay

his worry. The way she touches him still offers no clue as to their relation to one another. She waves Lyle away, and he moves past me, back to the kitchen. His face offers nothing on his thoughts of the encounter.

I slyly shift my weight to see around the back of the man's head, and spy the woman reassuring him. She smiles, and I see that she's distraught. For being so young, there's a sadness hanging on her, like a lead weight chained around her neck. She's scared, too. Not of the man, but of something else. The woman grabs her purse and ruffles through it, producing a small coin purse. As she plucks out a gleaming quarter, some of the other change spills out onto the table with a musical clatter. A rogue quarter rolls down the aisle and I slam my boot down on top of it.

The woman scoots off the bench and steps in front of the jukebox. She's looking to this machine to rescue her, salvage whatever it is that's in crisis.

The plastic pages flip behind that glass bubble, clack after clack. After a moment of indecisiveness, she stabs her finger at two of the buttons.

That's when she turns around and our eyes meet.

She gasps.

The man hears this and pivots in the booth. His eyes widen when he sees me, as if he's seeing a ghost.

It's dead silent now.

Without taking her eyes off of me, the woman stumbles back into the booth. She looks even more scared than she did before. Horrified, even. She scurries across from the man in a hurry, hiding from me.

Where there would normally be the tick of a clock, or voices, there is nothing.

Why were they looking at me like that?

Why won't anyone talk to me?

Why is everyone acting so bizarre?

Just as these questions begin to drive my anxiety to a darker place, the woman's selected tune comes on, scratchy and haunting.

"Be my baby," by The Ronettes.

My skin goes cold. My eyes fill with tears.

This is my favorite song. It always was. Ivy and I used to listen to it, over and over again. We'd put it on repeat, listen to it for hours in our bedroom. We used to twist the dial on the volume to the max, hoping to flush our parents out of hiding. We thought maybe they'd come to punish us. Scream and yell. Destroy the cassette player. Ground us for two weeks without television.

But no.

They never came.

They'd just let it play out, like letting a baby cry for hours on end without contact. Letting us adapt to our solitary environment. Our solitary lives. *Their* solitary lives, more specifically.

Except for Father and Ivy's special time together, of course.

The itch under my skin begins to scurry as I think about the red door and Ivy and Father. I think about laying in bed watching the hour hands tick by, wondering what went on behind that door. I used to hear her through the air conditioner vent. Crying. Whimpering.

Afraid.

They sounded so far away sometimes I thought I'd imagined them. Heard these horrible sounds in my sleep.

"Be my little baby."

Then I'd wake up, much later, and Ivy would be there again. She would be there, and I'd reach a hand out to wipe her tears away while I held her and she cried. I cried, too. It still feels like a dream.

The song ends with a deep scratch and when I look up again, the couple is gone.

It's just me again.

I get up, walk over to the jukebox, put another quarter in, and play it again.

A new couple has replaced the old one.

The man is tall, just like the one before. There's a sharp quality to his face. The symmetry in his features are like the blade of a knife. Clear. Defined. But he's not dangerous, just dedicated to a higher purpose. His mind has transcended this town, and his family, but his body couldn't go with it.

At least that's what *I* see.

The woman is older, unlike the one from earlier. She holds a pen in one hand, a crossword puzzle in the other. Her hair is pulled back in a tight bun, and she has a string of elegant pearls around her throat.

There's two more at their table.

Children. Two girls.

While the other couple barely smiled, this one doesn't smile at all. They're the victims of too many thoughts. The suggestion of too many ideas. Too complex even for themselves.

Before long I realize that I'm seeing a table of ghosts. A living memory playing out before my very eyes.

I remember hearing once that people often attract one another based on their levels of intelligence. If that really is true, then it makes sense how they ended up together. Intellect can often hinder the ability to communicate, and in their case, it created this invisible wall so they could never really see each other under the surface. That's often what I think happened to them. They paired off the way animals do, the way a lioness will adopt a male for protection. They married, but never really understood what to do afterwards. They just sort of "existed" together, rather than becoming an entity.

I see us here in that corner booth, thinking back on those ritualistic Friday nights at the diner.

I am just eight years old. Ivy is a mere seven.

This is our typical Friday night. One of our family's only means of escape, and virtually the only time we spend together aside from nightly suppers at home. I believe they use such occasions as a means to an end, that they parade us around every Friday evening so that the town doesn't suspect anything sinister. Because if people know Ivy and I are alive, how on earth could anything possibly be wrong?

The people of Silvers Hollow smile. They wave. Shake hands with my mother and father as we pass them in the plaza and on the sidewalks. My parents have become very good at faking smiles. At making people believe that they're normal. They're like politicians, really.

"Father?" little me says.

Father looks down at me, his eyes sharp as a hawk. Mother doesn't lift her eyes from her crossword puzzle.

"Ivy wants to try something new this time," I say.

Ivy was shy, *painfully* shy. At one point, we all thought that maybe she couldn't talk. But eventually, she did. Although she might as well not have, because she hardly says anything nowadays. I think maybe it's her way of getting back at our mother and father. Because of what was happening to her. To our family.

The only times I'd hear her speak was when she was in pain. I think before long I preferred her to be silent, because every time she *did* speak, it meant that something horrible was happening under our roof. Right beside all of those pretend smiles and waves.

I had to speak on her behalf. My parents despised this, I could tell.

"Ivy wants something different," I say.

Father looks at little me curiously. "Is that so?"

That same shiver from before makes my arms prickle with goosebumps.

I nod.

"She can tell me that herself," he says. There's no real clear tone to his voice. I can't tell if he's irritated, or amused, or angry. He's very mechanical.

"You know she can't."

"Can't, or won't?" he asks.

Father's eyes slide over to Ivy, then back to me. His mouth curls into a smile. "Fine, then."

I know this smile. This is what he does. Nothing was given for free in our home. Everything had to be earned. Since we were too young to work, Father insisted on making us earn our keep in other ways. Mainly through lateral thinking puzzles, riddles, or other challenges to test our cognitive thinking.

"Fine," Father says. "You answer correctly and Ivy can order whatever she would like. A Root Beer float. Banana Split. Cherry Pie. Anything. You as well."

Cherry pie was Ivy's favorite.

I suspect that long before Ivy and I ever knew, they both saw that we would never live up to their standards, never be the legacy that they wanted to leave behind. It would make sense, then, why they never wanted anything to do with us. Because of all their profound, unspoken disappointment. And in that vein, I used every single opportunity to show them that they were wrong. That I *was* everything they were, and so much more, because I actually understood that there was another side to the world. The one they never saw, never could see. Because their life was one without color, without dreams, and without hope—as barren as the surface of the Moon. The same moon Father looked at every night through his telescope.

"Fine."

Father turns to Mother. She looks at him and then her eyes fall back to her paper.

Father looks at me, as if my answer to this riddle will determine the outcome of whatever is left to be had.

As if nothing else matters.

Little me rises to the challenge with a tip of her head. There are very few I haven't been able to solve. "I'm ready," she says bravely.

Father smiles, then says, "When you are with me, you are lost in pages of madness, among fragments of broken images and false promises, lies and savage deceits. They often appear in a well of darkness, and stretch across time, an eternity yet somehow fleeting. As these images appear, they are logical, but later, upon recollection, they are odd, suspect," he says. He narrows his eyes at me, intense and unwavering. "What am I?"

Little me stares across at him, unblinking. Her hand tightens around Ivy's, and Ivy glares at him because she knows we've beaten him.

And without fear, little me says, "A dream."

Dreams.

I remember sitting with Ivy in the backyard in my mother's garden one warm summer afternoon. We'd found this box of old clothes in the garage and decided to play dress up, piecing together costumes with the silliest scraps we could find. We wanted to pretend we were someone else, wanted to get lost in this lovely fantasy and just...escape.

Adults would just take a vacation. But as kids, you don't have that luxury. Who you end up with is something you have absolutely no control over. You can end up with the greatest, most loving people in the world, or someone much, much worse.

The thing of it is, people often forget that under the right circumstances, dreams *are* an escape. As I entered adolescence, I began to notice that I was able to frequently "lucid dream," which is basically when you're aware that you're dreaming. Thousands of people experience this phenomenon, but don't really know or understand what's happening. Things can become so real. So fantastic and wonderful and magical. But the best part of all of that? Control. You are in control of everything that's happening around you. I would trade out one reality for another, and for me, that became *my* escape. I looked forward to going to sleep, anticipated that time when my eyes would close and I'd go somewhere else, far away from Silvers Hollow. Away from my parents. Away from the worries and fears I had at home.

This continued for years and never really stopped. The older I became, the better I got at controlling my dreams.

The trick is awareness. The more aware you are of what's happening around you, the easier it is to know you're in the dream world. And at the height of my dream domination, I was lucid dreaming virtually every night. That is until one night.

Winterview City.

Winterview is the nearest metropolitan city to Silvers Hollow. It has a population of approximately 2,500,000 people. At least, it did. I'd been there many times growing up, as I said before. Ivy and I were frequent visitors to Winterview. There's a train that tethers the two cities. The same one that left me here.

I had been staying at a premiere hotel in Winterview by chance. There was an emergency meeting called by the board of directors for Father's company, so I wanted to make myself accessible should they come up with any ridiculous excuses to use against me, like saying I wasn't in attendance or some nonsense.

By this time in my life I had been in hundreds of hotels, including some of the most renowned in the world. The Plaza. The Burj Al Arab in Dubai (a personal favorite). The Ritz. The Beverly Hills Hotel.

The establishment was nothing special in comparison. It has unremarkable paintings of ships lost at sea. Hideous gray paisley wallpaper. A floor-length mirror on the wall with a jagged crack running through it. Why they haven't replaced it is beyond me.

All of the furniture was white. The leather club chair in the corner. The bedspread. The Crown molding. There was something unsettling about the layout. The dark walls and floor clashed with the ultra-modern white furniture, yet somehow they complemented each other perfectly.

I'd awoken in that room in Winterview. It was fall. My Father had manipulated me into working for his company. He knew that by this time my face was everywhere, and that people would trust me.

I heard a mechanical sound, electrical-like, beyond the

window. Sort of like a charge. Everything was blurry. My eyes were heavy, my body turned to a lead weight.

I rolled over and noticed a red stain pooled around my stomach. At first I didn't think anything of it. I think maybe it's part of the bedspread, because I'm only utilizing a fraction of my mind in this sluggish state.

But, no. This is a white bedspread. There are no patterns on this comforter.

This realization startles me. I recoil and peel my shirt off my stomach to find nothing but iced, sweat-glazed skin.

No holes.

No cuts.

No wounds at all.

At least none that are visible.

I dig through the mess of sheets and the comforter and find a wine glass.

I thought I left it on the end table next to my medication.

The glass is empty.

I must have fallen asleep and spilled it.

My eyes begin to feel heavy again. The world is

swaying.

And then I hear that sound again.

A distant crash beyond the window. A hiss of electricity. There's a noticeable hum. A charge.

It's faint, and I can't tell if it's real, or just my imagination.

Dark curtains are drawn to the side of the window, but the sheers shield me from whatever is on the other side.

I shuffle from bed, setting the wine glass down on the end table next to a bottle of pills. I head for the bathroom.

As my feet meet the cold tile I notice there's a haze of mist crawling over my skin. I feel it like someone's breath, raspy and chilled.

I flip the switch.

The light explodes on overhead.

All around the medicine cabinet and walls are dozens of vines. They snake around the doorframe like veins. I suddenly feel like I'm inside myself. I see arteries and blood and chambers of sinew.

I turn toward the mirror only to find a blurry, distorted figure staring back at me.

It's one of the most horrible things I've ever seen. There's a malevolence there, in that mirror, that I recognize. This disturbing form has taken my identity and turned it to a thousand burned leaves. A face with no face.

A scream begins to climb in my throat, and just before I can call out, a blinding white light explodes beyond the window with a deep bass sound, like a hundred trumpets.

I can't tell if it's me screaming, or rather the city itself, and it is only then that I decide that it doesn't matter if this is a dream, because whatever is outside that window, is going to change my life.

The world seems darker now than it did an hour ago. I've missed my appointment. I'm sure of it. Maybe I *am* trying to self-sabotage?

After leaving the Nighthawk Diner, I've managed to find the Psychologist's office. It's tucked away down one of the side streets that connects to the main plaza. It really is like a different world back here.

Whereas jangly lights trace the rooftops out in the plaza, on this street, there is nothing. Just shadows and cobblestone with dreary windows.

This doesn't look like the front of a doctor's office. It reminds me more of somewhere you'd go to be sewn up for a gunshot wound while trying to avoid the hospitals. There's a single door recessed into the brick. No windows. No sign. Only an address. The same one that was written on the card.

The door is bright red; it looks identical to the one from our house. The one that leads to the basement. It makes me uncomfortable, looking at it. Just the thought of opening it brings tremors to my hands.

This isn't my home, though. This is somewhere completely different.

I'm safe here. Aren't I?

Just above the address, there's a lantern. The light has a tint the color of a fine merlot, like it's being fed by the color of the red door. A couple of moths are beating around it. They look peaceful, fluttering off the glass panes. One of them has found its way inside.

It's trapped.

The moths bounce off the glass housing with weighty little thumps. I hold out my hand and one of them lands on top. I watch it for a moment before it flutters away, into the night.

I take a deep breath and twist the knob. The heavy door slams behind me, and I look around to make sure I haven't disturbed anyone. It's deafly quiet in here.

I'm in the waiting room.

I hear the mechanical tap of keys.

The seats lining the walls are empty. I glance at the magazine rack. Vogue. True Detective. Life. All familiar for the most part. Only with these magazines, the covers don't match what I remember; the art is something from an older time.

More typing. It jabs at me from the other end of the room.

A plump woman in a cardigan watches me from behind a desk. She has dark eyes covered by oversized glasses that have a little jeweled chain hanging around her neck. Like some type of accountant, or bookkeeper. In front of her there's an old-fashioned typewriter, the kind before keyboards and computers and Internet Explorer.

"Hello," she says. Her smile is crooked; one side of her mouth hangs lower than the other, as if her jaw has been broken sometime in the past and never healed correctly. Or maybe she had a stroke?

I approach the counter.

"Good evening," I greet.

The woman cocks her head oddly. The tapping on the keys turns to silence.

The woman says, "You're right on time."

"I am?"

The woman's smile holds unnaturally. "Indeed. The doctor has been expecting you."

"She has?"

"Yes."

We stand looking at each other for a moment, then she says, "Before your appointment, please fill out this short questionnaire." She hands me a clipboard with a pen attached with one of those little chains.

I half smile. "Thanks."

As I take a seat in one of the chairs, I say, "Do you happen to have the time?"

The receptionist lifts her eyes over the lenses and says, "No."

I gave it a shot.

I look down at the form. There are dozens of questions. If I'm a patient here, shouldn't they already have this information?

"Excuse me?" I say.

The typing stops again. The receptionist looks up. She doesn't appear to be annoyed by me. She almost looks relieved that I'm speaking to her. Like she'd rather be talking to me than thinking about whatever's on her mind.

"Don't you already have this information? I'm a returning patient." A pause, then: "Aren't I?"

She looks unimpressed. Like I've asked a librarian where the comic book section is. "Not all of our information has been transferred since the move. Some of our patient files are still in transit. Emergency and all."

The move? That would explain why this office is a ghost town.

"In transit?" I mutter.

She nods. "Yes. I'm afraid many services have been suspended as of late. Until they arrive, we have to insist on patients filling out their paperwork."

The emergency again? This is the second time now

she's mentioned this "emergency."

I shift in my seat with a confused flutter of my eyes. I tap the pen on the clipboard as I chew my lip. Out of the corner of my eye I can see she's still watching me.

Finally, I exhale and it's almost like a laugh. Almost like this entire night has been so ridiculous and absurd that I can't *help* but laugh.

The receptionist isn't laughing, however. She's the complete opposite of funny. She's stone-faced. Deathly serious. "Are you all right, Miss?" she asks.

"I'm sorry," I say. "I just…" my voice trails off.

"Miss?"

"*What* emergency?" I say with a shrug.

The receptionist's frosty expression falls heavy with sympathy. Her eyes begin to well with tears. She begins to sob lightly before pulling a handkerchief from her pocket and dabbing her eyes. Clearly she's upset about something.

The scent of guilt is heavy now on me. "Are *you* all right?" I ask.

"Yes, yes, of course," she says. She takes a deep breath as she fights to regain her composure.

"Ma'am?" I say. I hold my hands up, as if to say *what's on your mind?*

She looks at me as though she's completely forgotten what I've asked. "The emergency?" I repeat.

I see fear blossom in her eyes. They widen at the words, triggered by an internal alarm. And then she says, "The doctor will be with you shortly."

I've filled out dozens of these medical questionnaires. While you may have assumed that Mother and Father didn't care much about our wellbeing, they were in actuality strangely unmatched when it came to our healthcare. *Obsessed* is a better word. I don't think I ever missed a doctor's appointment growing up. Father didn't trust any of the doctors in Silvers Hollow (he said it was far too small a town for any real talent), so he would take it upon himself to drive us as far as he needed to make sure our health was immaculate. Whether rain or shine, he'd make sure I was there.

But now that I think back, I don't actually recall Ivy

and I going together. Ivy and Father had their own trips. They'd leave together, be gone for hours at a time. Just like with the basement. At such a young age, I don't think I ever really understood what was happening. Never questioned why she was gone and he was gone and I was left home with Mother or more often by myself. A note of resentment festered under my skin like a disease. I secretly hated them both for leaving me behind. For having their own little secret life that I wasn't a part of.

Now that we're on the topic, I don't ever recall them *leaving* together, either. They'd just both be gone. I'd wake up and go looking for Ivy, and when I couldn't find her, I'd look for Father.

Instead, I'd find Mother. She'd be in the kitchen at the table, or in the office, a collection of file folders splayed in front of her.

"Where's Father?" I'd ask.

"He had to go to the city for supplies," she'd say.

"And Ivy?"

Mother would look at me sadly. Almost like she pitied me. She did this just long enough to make me feel inadequate.

"You're too old to be doing this."

Have you suffered from any recent hallucinations or fits of epilepsy?

What kinds of questions are these, anyway?

I still don't know what I'm doing here. Don't know why I came at all. I've never seen a psychologist before. I've never *needed* a psychologist. While I'd argue that they have me confused with someone else, the receptionist does claim to recognize me.

She seems to have calmed down for now. She's gone back to her typing. On a *typewriter* mind you. Not a Mac. Not a Dell, or HP. A typewriter. Like the ones Ernest

Hemingway and Agatha Christie used. The oldest computers I remember using had that old game *The Oregon Trail* on them. You remember: the same one that would tell you that you died of dysentery. Or a snakebite. Or that your whole family drowned in the Kansas River. I remember wondering when I was older if the little people in the game would have gone mad if their entire family had died. Would they have had survivor's guilt? How much longer would they have stuck around until they couldn't live with themselves anymore? Until they decided that maybe it was better to be dead rather than to go on living without the people that mattered to them most?

This typewriter. The tapping. It makes the cogs in my mind come to life—makes them grind.

Either this practice is really in trouble after the so-called "emergency," or they don't believe in technology.

Have you been treated by a physician or hospitalized in the last year?

Ugh. How many more of these are there? I feel that same itch under the soft skin of my forearm. My nails carve red welts into it, sawing back and forth.

Why does it feel like there's something inside? Buried beneath my skin?

Are you currently taking any prescription medication or anti-psychotics?

It's surprising how invasive these seemingly innocent questionnaires are. The psychologist is making everyone fill these out before she'll see them. Isn't that cheating somehow? Shouldn't *she* be the one asking me these questions?

I should just mark NO for all of them. They claim that I'm a patient here, so clearly she should know these things about me.

Or maybe she's lying. Maybe the receptionist is lying? But why lie? What purpose would that serve?

Have you ever experienced emotional or physical abuse as child?

The pen stops.

The typing stops.

The sounds cease.

During childhood, I preferred to pretend that things like "abuse" didn't exist. That it was impossible that somewhere, someone was experiencing something horrible that I couldn't stop. That it could never happen to me, or Ivy. That my parents weren't capable of anything like that.

Instead, I preferred to believe that we just *were*. We were there with Mother and Father living with these strange little idiosyncrasies within our family that I never really understood.

But I adapted. I was the chameleon. The invisible champion. The one who would be there when the dust settled to show them that I didn't need them any more than they needed me.

My mind drifts through the darkest parts of space, past dimming stars and lost dreams and arrives at the red door.

There are little scratches all around the ticker box because I'm trembling.

It's then that I see the entire area around the checkbox. It's covered in erratic scratches from the sharp tip of the pen.

I've marked the wrong box.

octor Aurora Snow. Psychologist extraordinaire.

The only thing is, there's nothing really "psychologist" about her. When I think of a shrink, I see a woman in a pantsuit holding a notebook, jotting down chicken scratch whenever I say something that snags her attention. Maybe some witty remark about my childhood? Maybe how I was mad at my mother for never helping me pick out a dress for prom?

So far, there is no pantsuit. No notebook. No drivel.

We've hardly said two words since I've come into the room.

Her office is sterile. Unintentionally, it seems. Off in the corner there's a splintered wooden ladder and a roller next to a bucket of paint. The space reminds me of a room at the looney ward where people wear straitjackets and take medication at exactly one o'clock in the afternoon from a little plastic cup.

What Dr. Snow *is*, is unfamiliar. Just like I thought. I've never met this woman. I'm certain of it. She does seem like some sort of professional business type; I just can't place what kind. Being one myself, I can spot them a mile away. These people have a certain air about them, as if they're a beacon for power. Commanding figures. Imposing without being *too* threatening. Politicians. CEOs. Surgeons. Detectives. The type of person that can see right through you. Can see through a lie. Make you question yourself. I have no doubt that the woman in front of me can manipulate virtually anyone into doing anything.

Speaking to her has an upside, of course. People like this are great at helping you see the things you're hiding. Especially the ones you're hiding from yourself.

"It's been some time," she starts.

I nod slowly.

"I was worried you weren't going to come. It's good to see you again."

Worried. Give me a break. This woman couldn't care less if I was on fire right on her fancy leather couch.

"What's the matter?" she asks.

"Nothing. Why do you ask?"

"I saw you on the news," she says.

There it is again. Someone else that saw me on TV. So it isn't that I recognize *her*, it's that she recognizes *me*.

"You were very inspirational," she says with a sly smile. "You've always been a natural with public speaking. Even when you were younger."

I feel myself blush, and I smile at her. I can't help it. It's a reflex. Ever since the first time I was on television, I've been enamored by the experience. People would come up to me on the streets and shower me with praise, tell me how lovely I was. As if I was Marilyn Monroe or some starlet with sparkling white teeth. In retrospect, I think I was starved for all the attention I never got when I was a child.

But this quack obviously hasn't made the connection despite her field of expertise.

Dr. Snow sees my response and takes the opportunity to bring me down a couple of notches from my pedestal. "Of course, it's been some time since then. A lot has changed in the world. For the worse, unfortunately." She pauses, watching my reaction, then says, "I'm sorry about what happened."

So cryptic. I can't help but wonder if all psychologists talk in code. I surmise it's part of the reason they get into this profession in the first place. Solving the puzzle that is the human mind.

"How have you been feeling lately?" she asks.

I shrug, leaning forward in the chair. "Fine, really." Best to keep these answers short or this is liable to go on forever.

"That's good," she replies. "Everything that's happening outside of this town...well...let's just say not everyone is handling it quite as well as you. Not well at all, in fact."

I am?

Handling what?

The sleeve of my jacket is pulled up and she sees the scratches. We make eye contact. She doesn't comment, just waits for me to address them.

"It's a rash. Bug bite, or something. It's been driving me crazy," I say, tugging my sleeve down to cover it. "Itches like hell."

"Huh," she says.

Very insightful, this woman.

"Would you like to talk about why you're here?"

"Why I'm here?"

"Yes."

"In the office?"

She nods.

What in the world is this woman talking about?

She sees the confusion on my face and fills in the blanks. "You made this appointment, but we've had to delay it a couple of times," she explains.

Why would we need to delay it?

She continues. "You said you were worried—about Ivy. About what was going to happen."

Ivy.

So she *does* know me.

"What about her?" I ask.

"Have you spoken to your Father?"

I shake my head.

"May I ask why?"

"He *knows* why."

"Ah, I see," she answers. "And you're still angry with them?" she says rhetorically.

A flurry of musical jackpot bells ring out in my head. Lucky guesser, this one.

"You still hold him responsible," she asks, "for what happened?"

"You know I do." I practically growl the words.

"You've been away a very long time. On your twentieth birthday you left their service and went out on your own, into the world. Made a life for yourself, away from all those...memories."

I have to give her credit. Her little observations dig at me more than I want to admit. They're jabs without jabbing. Pain without the affliction.

Dr. Snow leans forward in her chair and steeples her fingers. Her eyes are like a lake. Silver. Painfully clear. Cold. She stares at me with the most intense stare I've ever seen. She leans forward in her chair and says, "Why have you come back to Silvers Hollow?"

What a waste of time. I've left Dr. Snow's office with more questions than answers.

The only thing she's been successful with is bringing my blood to the boiling point.

The longer I'm away from there, the more I'm convinced there's something off about Dr. Snow. About the receptionist. About this town.

She's not wrong, though.

What *am* I doing here?

This isn't amnesia. I haven't forgotten anything. I remember my birthday. I remember our address. My career. I remember Ivy. Father. Mother. My life. Yet somehow, rather inexplicably, I don't remember what I'm doing back in this town.

The thought drives itself like a needle behind my eye. A tiny thing that's somehow incredibly painful. Piercing.

I step out the front door to the office and find the alley bathed in a red cyclone. The light lashes over the backstreet, paints the decrepit walls crimson.

The cycling is somehow worse than when it was just darkness back here. This feels more immediate. Dangerous. Like I've just walked onto a crime scene.

I turn to find the same antique police cruiser from before parked just a short way down the alley. Officer Smith is standing in front of the wall. He has one hand on his hip, the other on his gun.

He's staring at the wall. Just staring.

I slowly approach, careful not to startle him.

But I do anyway.

He twists his head toward me but doesn't draw his weapon.

At first there's relief on his face. He looks at me with lost eyes, then shakes his head.

"What's going on?" I ask.

He begins to raise his hands in a lazy effort to shoo me away but gives up halfway through. This has become our routine.

As I step closer, the darkness in front of Officer Smith begins to twist into shape. The blackness begins to manifest before my eyes.

The wall; it's covered in blood. Or something resembling blood. The slick is smeared over the concrete crudely. The macabre art reminds me of the work of a cult.

Wait.

Was this here before? Did I walk right past it on my way to the appointment? Or did it appear while I was talking with Dr. Snow? It was so dark it's hard to know for certain.

I'm too shaken to speak, so I just stand with Officer Smith and take it all in.

Without warning, the insufferable itch in my forearm returns with a vengeance. Only the prickling is everywhere. It scurries along my skin, creeping in and out of the crevices of my body.

Officer Smith misinterprets that I'm uncomfortable by the symbols on the wall and says, "Miss? You shouldn't be looking at this." He begins to walk toward me but I ignore him and step closer to it.

I'm hypnotized by the sight. I can't take my eyes off of it. You hear about things like this happening in the real world. Animals slaughtered in rituals. Corpses found with images carved into their flesh. But I've never seen it firsthand.

My left eye begins to twitch. It feels like there's something inside. I picture a tiny white worm slithering through the liquid inside. Coiling. Trying to get out.

"Miss?" Officer Smith says again.

His voice grounds me. The itching stops. My thoughts go blank.

I crane my neck and he's gazing at me.

"Who did this?" I ask.

"I don't know." Officer Smith says grimly. "Someone reported it. About an hour ago. Someone's idea of a sick joke."

I say, "It doesn't look like a joke to me."

Officer Smith reluctantly nods in agreement.

He's scared. Far more scared than I would think a policeman would be in his situation. There's no doubt this is disturbing, but to a veteran of the force it's surprising to see. He's almost more afraid than I am.

Behind him, where the alley curves away into a tunnel of blackness, I see movement.

His face falls into a blur and another shape develops into focus.

I nearly suffer a meltdown by this point. Nowhere in my mind can logic rationally explain what I'm seeing right now.

Officer Smith is too taken by the grisly artwork to notice. But *I* see it. Just waiting. Watching us from the opposite end of the alley.

There's a tiger.

Not a lion. Not a cougar, or panther. Not a leopard or jaguar. A tiger. A real-life tiger. The kind with the burnt orange fur and black stripes.

I know how it sounds, but it's there. Even though it's infinitely dark outside, I can tell. The animal is easily five hundred pounds or more. It's just watching us from the end of the alley. Pacing back and forth. Like it's waiting to be fed.

Its primal black eyes find my own, and I shudder.

Am I really seeing this? How is this possible?

My breathing slows as it watches me. I don't move. *Can't* move.

Meanwhile, Officer Smith is oblivious. I want to warn him. Want to shout and scream and tell him what's there, watching us. But I can't. What if it hears me? What if it hears and comes for us? I've seen what these things can do.

The tiger stares at me and I stare back. Neither of us gives an inch. If I take my eyes off it, there's a chance it could charge us. It would be ripping out my throat before Officer Smith could get the gun out of his holster.

And just when I've worked up enough courage to whisper to him, the tiger stops, tilts its head, then slinks back into the darkness.

I think back to my first conversation with Officer Smith. The worry he was drenched in. But it's starting to make sense now, because there's something horribly wrong with this town.

And I'm starting to understand why he said it isn't safe.

I 've had enough. This is the final straw. I can't spend another second in this town. Finding a phone has become my number one priority.

Officer Smith has taken me prisoner in his back seat. Again. So far he's offered me nothing in the way of reassurances. I should also mention that he now thinks I'm insane. You see, in a moment of unadulterated stupidity, I've told him about the tiger.

Why? Because I assumed this man was decent enough not to assume I was a raving lunatic. It *does* sound a smidge crazy, though, doesn't it? A tiger lurking around a small town in Connecticut. There are big cats in the woods, of course. Bobcats. The occasional mountain lion. But tigers? Those exotic cats with the bright orange fur? No. Maybe at the zoo. But I've never been. Our parents never took us to the zoo on daytrips like normal families.

But worse than that, I've attempted twice now to shift the spotlight to the scene we just came from. But even despite what we've just seen, he's acting like it's no big deal.

"What do you think they mean?" I ask. "The symbols?"

He shakes his head. "Nothing. Just nonsense. Like I said, probably someone's idea of a joke. Nothing more." He has no conviction as he says this.

That's fine, though. If he doesn't want to tell me what's going on, he doesn't have to. Lord knows I can't force him.

"Listen, what we saw back there…"

I wait.

Then he says, "Keep it between us. I don't want folks panicking."

I watch the strings of lights of the town plaza slowly brighten the car. Bright, then dark. Bright. Dark. Bright.

Dark.

"What were you doing outside, anyway?" Officer Smith asks. "I thought I told you to stay inside?"

I scoff.

"You got something to say?" he says.

"Am I under arrest?"

Officer Smith exhales sharply.

"Then why are you driving me around?"

"Well, I—"

"No. It's a simple question. YES, or NO?"

He pulls over to the curb and cuts the engine. He glances at me in the mirror, then turns, resting his arm along the top of the seats. "Things aren't that simple here."

"Meaning?"

"Meaning you are a *guest* in this town. Whoever you were before you came here, doesn't matter to me. You may be some big shot back in the city, but in *my* town, you're no better than anyone else, and I will treat you as such."

Well, that answers that. He recognizes me too, apparently. It shouldn't be a surprise, but it is. I'm sure the majority of the world has seen me multiple times by this point. I guess I just figured they'd forget. Forget my face. Forget me. Forget what I did.

What I did?

"Whatever it is that's bothering you," he says, "you better get over it *quick*. There are much bigger things happening here than you realize. And I don't have the time to be worrying about you all fuckin' night."

I glare at him in the rearview mirror.

"I do, however, understand that you're going through something…well…something extraordinary. In fact, I can say the same for the majority of the townsfolk. But lady, to be honest, I ain't got the time."

I look across the plaza for the single red Mustang from before. It's gone. The world suddenly feels a little lonelier.

Officer Smith continues, "Fortunately for you, I'm a good friend of your father's."

"You're a liar."

"What did you just say, young lady?"

"My father doesn't have friends."

"Couple folks are havin' a little get-together soon. Some sort of dinner."

Then, he says, "Kind man that I am, I have taken it upon myself to make sure you are first on the guest list."

"A party?" Okay. This is too weird. I can't imagine a party in any capacity in this town. I can't fathom what that would even look like.

"After the day you've had, I would think you could use a little fun. What do you say?"

When I don't answer, he grumbles and says, "I'm not asking anymore. You either stay inside, or next time I see you, you're gonna be spending the night in a jail cell."

"Stay inside *why*?" I ask. "What's going on? Why is nobody allowed outside?"

Officer Smith looks away. He can't face me. Either because he's ashamed of what he's doing or because he's afraid. I don't have to wait long to find out which.

"Look at me," I demand. "Look me in the eye and tell me *why* I can't go out. Where the hell is everybody? What was that on the wall back there?"

"Cut the bullshit, okay?" he asks. "You *know* what it is. And you know exactly what it means."

Finally, he lifts his eyes enough for me to see that he's

tired. Tired of arguing. He's getting no enjoyment out of this conversation. Obviously, his mind has more important things to worry about, and I believe him. "We don't want people to go outside…because…of… the…emergency." His voice is vacant. He's checked out.

There is it. Right on cue. The goddamn emergency.

Again.

How many times is it now that I've heard about this "emergency"?

Before I can respond, before I can let all of this wrath explode out of me, I freeze. My eyes narrow, squinting at Officer Smith in the moonlight.

"What?" he asks, noticing the curious look I'm giving him. His hand instinctively goes to his hair, thinking it's messed up. He rakes his fingers through the greasy strands.

"Your mustache," I say. "It's falling off."

Time. I mentioned that not having my watch irks me, but it's more than that. Unnerves is a better word for it. It *unnerves* me, the not knowing part. The people that inhabit today's world would probably grasp this concept easier than you'd think. Take someone's phone, hide it, then watch. Five minutes without a phone is liable to give someone a panic attack. It's like an invisible IV of digital drugs. A lifeline. For me, it's not a missing phone that does it. It's my watch. I didn't say why.

Father had a job like any other dad. He went to work from nine to five like other dads (although often stayed much later since he was on call). Shaved and showered every morning. Enjoyed throwing a sirloin on the grill Saturdays. He even waxed his car, and Mother's. But that's where the similarities ended.

You see, Father had these things about him that were different than other parents.

He didn't watch football. Didn't spend his days off building birdhouses or mowing the lawn (we had a gardener for the lawn—two, in fact).

More specifically, he was something of a horologist. Not in the literal sense of the word. But that's the closest thing I can compare it to. Father was *obsessed* with time. Where some people had religion and God, Father had time.

One time I walked into his office in an attempt to get him to take Ivy and I to the park.

"Father?" I'd said.

Father looked up from his desk, where dozens of papers and notes were scribbled all over. He was out of breath, like he'd just run a marathon in his mind.

He looked at me, kind of like he didn't recognize me. That's how deep he would get. How far he'd go when he was focusing on something.

"I was wondering; could we maybe go to the park today? You and Mother and Ivy and me?"

"And *I*," Father corrected.

I'd watched as he sifted through the information like a computer. "Does not compute." That's the phrase that came to mind at times like this.

"It's just...it's such a nice day outside," little me said.

"Did you know that the average lifespan is 22,075,000 seconds?"

I didn't know what to say, so I just said, "No."

"That is all we get, and then, well...we're gone. Our bodies decompose. Our bones eventually turn to dust."

Little me just stared at him.

"Stardust. That's all we really are," he'd said.

"We just want to go out. Like a family. Like a *real* family. Ivy and I—"

"That's enough about Ivy. *Quite* enough."

"Why can't she ever go with us to the park?"

"We've talked about this before."

"But why?"

"Because," he snapped. "You're content living in a fantasy." He paused. "I don't understand it... Can't understand it. But the rest of us—we have to live *here*. In reality. Where there's time. And rules. And time tells us what we can and can't do. Not me."

Father pointed at a clock hanging on the wall with his pen and said, "Take note. You've just taken that much more time from me *and* yourself."

"What do you do in the basement?" The words cut through the air like a blade. "With Ivy?"

My father ceased writing, then turned to look up at me, disgust written on his face. He exhaled, taken aback, like he was genuinely shocked I knew.

"Something you would never understand."

The one thing Father used to tell me about death? Your hair keeps growing.

Only, that's not really true at all. It's a misconception. A misnomer. The reality is grimmer. What actually happens is your skin recedes, pulls away from your fingernails and your teeth, so you look more like some deranged version of who you used to be. Those same pearly white teeth that usually make smiles heavenly turn people into terrifying monsters.

But that hair thing always gets to me; it has since I was a kid. We'd just left the funeral when Father offered up that bit of trivia. Some might have found it distasteful, but

I didn't. We were used to the way his mind worked by then. Understood him to a point. He just said what was on his mind. Spoke his thoughts without a filter. One of the few qualities I appreciated about him. We didn't have to tiptoe around each other's feelings.

I'm back at the house, sitting in an uncomfortable recliner in the living room. I run my fingers through my hair. The silk is gone. In its place? Grease. I can't help but think how bad I must look right now. On normal occasions, I keep up appearances well. I take time to get my fingers and toes manicured. Go to the best salons in the world to see to my highlights. Wear the finest fabrics and only consume the healthiest foods. My jewelry is elegant, but tasteful. I exercise, maybe drink a glass of white wine with dinner. That tuna sandwich was the first thing I've eaten in years that was marginally unhealthy.

The point is, I take care of myself. Take pride in my appearance. To me, grooming is a reflection of the person. And in my humble opinion, a person who looks like hell usually isn't that well put together.

But I am.

At least, I was. Right now I don't feel like myself. Ever since the train literally left the station, I've felt like someone else. Like I was living someone else's life. This feels more like a dream every second. Where everything I see is an illusion. The blood in the alley. The tiger. The little green gift box. The jukebox. Officer Smith and his mustache. The woman watering her fake lawn. The couple at the diner.

My family has no history of mental illness. I'm not sick. I'm not imagining this. It's happening. It's real. It has to be.

Doesn't it?

I'm in the kitchen now. I snatch the phone from its cradle. The curly cord is tangled. I fumble it in my hands, peeling it apart.

I hook a finger into the wheel and spin, dialing the first number that comes to mind. The rotary makes that little clicking sound as it spins.

No wonder these things aren't around anymore. They're painfully slow. One number, spin. Second number, spin. Repeat times five.

The other line begins to ring.

When I hear a click, my heart skips a beat. I assume they've picked up. I feel myself start to smile but freeze midway through.

It's not a person. Not at all. It's an automated message. "Due to the emergency, all calls outside the city are temporarily suspended," the voice says. "We apologize for the inconvenience. Please try your call again later."

Beyond the window, I see a flash of light. A second after, there's a colossal boom so loud it rocks the house. I'm instantly transported back to the hotel room in Winterview. I feel my body tense thinking about the light I saw there, outside the window.

Lightning?

The incessant itch in my arm returns. My nails scrape across my raw skin as I approach the front door.

There's another crash. It's closer. High above the house.

I reach for the knob.

Another flash beyond the window. It reminds me of a stick of dynamite exploding. Or some kind of massive firecracker. The throb of light beams in through the decorative cutout on the top of the door, blinding me. I recoil, pitching my face away.

The itching grows.

I twist the knob and slowly pull open the handle.

A strong gale intrudes on the house; it powers through the streets.

It's cold, but there's a heat, the type of heat a warm engine gives off.

There's a mist in the air. It's everywhere. Invading the street. Creeping across the lawn. Rolling over driveways. Smothering lawn sculptures.

As I step through the fog blanketing the lawn, I stop dead in the center and look to the sky above the house.

The wind picks up, tossing the mist in all directions. Where normally there would be leaves blowing there is nothing but the flutter of my greasy hair.

Weak pulses of light explode above Silvers Hollow like a quiet storm. They light up the darkness the way you see lightning light up a sea of clouds. There are dozens of massive shapes in that darkness.

PATRICK DELANEY

Clouds?

The electric thunder shrieks and quakes the world.
The noise is so overwhelming I can feel my teeth rattle.

There's a storm coming.

I've retreated back inside. As fate would have it, there's a dinner party on the agenda. I'm not going to be able to leave here. Not tonight. Or today. Not with the phones down.

The sounds outside have finally calmed. They've been replaced by the sound of rain. Only it's not calming the way rain is calming. It's erratic. Disturbing. This rain doesn't have that soothing thrum that puts you to sleep. Doesn't carry the relaxing quality you think of when you're tucked in bed, listening to it through the window pane.

This sounds different. It's uneven. Lazy. Like the water is falling harder in some places and not others. I don't even know how to describe it. It's just not normal.

A knock at the front door.

My eyes widen.

Who would be outside in this mess?

The knock is pleasant as far as knocks go. It isn't some infernal pounding. It's just a polite little rap on the door. As if there wasn't a rainstorm going on behind it.

Another knock.

And when I don't answer, they knock again.

Reluctantly, I move to the door. I stand in front of it, contemplating who could be on the other side. I put my ear to the door and listen but hear nothing.

Who knows I'm here?

No one.

With the exception of Officer Smith, of course.

When they knock a fourth time, I jerk the handle open.

A draft whirls past me, as if escaping from outside.

A tiny old woman stares up at me. I recognize her; it's the woman that was with the other couple at the diner that had departed right after I'd arrived.

Her eyeglass frames are huge. I haven't seen a pair like this in years. A pair of giant, prying eyes stare up at me. They're clouded with milky cataracts.

"Hello," the old woman says.

"Can I help you?" I ask.

"My name is Wilda. I'm your new neighbor."

"Oh, I'm sorry, I didn't know anyone moved in recently?"

Wilda smiles. "How funny. I was actually just telling George the same thing about you."

"George?"

"My husband."

"Oh."

"A friend of ours in the department reached out to us. He said you might be feeling a little...*isolated* since your arrival. Heaven knows I don't blame you. Downright eerie out."

Of course he did.

"We thought we'd invite you to a quiet dinner to celebrate our good fortune."

I try to sidestep the invitation. "Our good fortune?"

Wilda's smile spreads to cheek to cheek. "Of course, my dear. An abundance, wouldn't you say?" She pauses. "So, will you join us?"

"Oh, I'm sorry…I'm a little busy right now."

The woman looks past me into the house, then back at me, unimpressed.

I laugh artificially, knowing she's caught onto my lie. "I'm not dressed for—"

"Your attire is of no consequence," she says, deathly serious. "Not on this night."

Dinner parties.

  We're walking now. In the rain. We've gone the opposite direction of the plaza. I'm holding the umbrella over Wilda. Half of my body is soaked by the time we arrive at the gate. The sky has returned to blackness. The lights have ceased. The thunder has ceased. Now, there is only the rain.

  Wilda isn't really my neighbor. She claims she is, but I wouldn't consider her that. A neighbor usually lives within a five-house vicinity. Someone you see at least once a week, either in passing or for those block parties people used to have. Wilda lives at the end of the road.

At least that was my first thought. Then she proceeded to explain that we weren't going to *her* house at all. She's clever with her words, for an old woman. Semantics.

Beyond the gate, the house is a Tudor-style mansion. Even bigger than ours, although I wouldn't say our house was anywhere near "mansion-sized." But this...

"It's beautiful," I say.

Wilda doesn't seem to care that I'm getting drenched. There's an air of superiority about her. Perhaps it's a generational thing?

"I don't remember it," I say.

Wilda looks at me. "Why would you?"

"I grew up here, when I was young."

Wilda is taken aback. "Oh really? What a coincidence that you ended up back here now."

I gaze at the house's silhouette. It's quite impressive, even in the darkness. The structure has a roundabout driveway, with a three-tier fountain in the middle. The roof is all slanted gables and tall chimneys. The façade of the house is a collection of brick and decorative half-timbering, with dozens of dark windows. It reminds me of something out of a murder-mystery.

"Who lives here?" I ask.

"Not one for surprises, are you?"

I don't say anything, just listen to the patter of the rain on the umbrella.

"Well, let's get on with it, then," Wilda says, starting forward.

Wilda smiles perfunctorily at me. "We didn't expect to come but decided that we couldn't pass up the chance for a house in Silvers Hollow. Nearly impossible to get in here. Unless you know the right people, of course."

"When did you arrive?"

This is the first question I'm faced with upon entering the house.

Wilda's husband, George, is the same man I saw at the diner. He reminds me of the type that sits around in some elitist polished mahogany gentleman's club smoking expensive cigars. A tad curt, but polite and welcoming.

"George," a second woman says, "she just got here. You don't want to scare the poor thing off now, do you?"

The woman turns to me and smiles, offering her hand. She's older as well but seems more genuine than the others. "Welcome to our home. I'm Hildy," she says. A second man waddles through the doorway like a penguin. This is the man I saw speaking to Lyle at the Nighthawk Diner. "And this," Hildy says, "is my husband, Bernard."

"Ah, hello," Bernard says. "Quite the day we've had, wouldn't you say?"

"George, why don't you fix our guest a drink?" Wilda says. She looks at George with a strange glint in her eye.

George looks and me and nods. "Of course," he says, starting toward a bar tucked in the corner of the room.

"I'm fine, real—" I begin.

Wilda raises a hand, silencing me. "George makes the best cocktails in the world," she says. "It's a hobby he adopted after retirement. Never thought we'd be drinking as much as we have these past few months, but rest assured, you're in good hands."

George returns with a glass filled with a brown liquid and a wedge of orange cut into the side. There's this smirk on his face that's oddly familiar.

As he hands me the glass, I notice Hildy looks worried, peering out at the rain. She turns to us, and I don't know why, but there's something troubling in the way she's watching George as he hands me the glass.

That's when her eyes catch mine and I see them widen. The same way that foreign couple looked at me in the diner.

"Here you are, my dear," George says.

I take the glass from him and say, "Thank you."

Then, they're all just standing there, watching me. A silence falls over the room and all that's left is the rain and the storm beyond the windows.

I look at each of their faces. They're waiting for me to say something.

You could hear a pin drop in here. The silence is unbearable, and I can't take it anymore. "I haven't seen it rain like this in years."

The air is sucked from the room as the words leave my mouth. You'd think I'd just told them the world was ending.

I take in the alarm on their faces and raise the glass to my mouth. "Cheers."

Their faces are painted in white-hot fear. This bunch is sophisticated, but they're as far on the edge as they could possibly be without falling off. For some reason, I feel relieved seeing them afraid. Maybe because I'm not the only one here who's afraid anymore. After all, they say misery loves company. Maybe they're right.

I swallow the entirety of the drink and say, "You're right, that *is* good."

A cascade of bile violently wrenches free from my throat; my abdomen pulls so tight I feel like my ribcage might collapse in on itself. I have to suppress every urge I have to make a sound. I can't let them hear. Can't let them know that I don't trust them, that this drink they handed me could be anything. Poison. Drugs. This wouldn't be the first time a stranger tried to hand me a drink. It used to happen all the time when I'd frequent the clubs when I was younger. Fortunately, I possess enough common sense to know the dangers of being too trusting too quickly.

I lift my head from the toilet and wipe my mouth,

stepping over to the sink. As the brisk water chills my hands, I look up to find that there's no mirror on the wall, but rather a crude sheet of pine. The same kind you'd see on a house that's under construction.

How odd. No mirror? It must have gotten broken. I tug the hand towel free from the ring and begin drying my hands, wondering how I ended up here, with these people. These…strangers.

Outside the bathroom, the hallway is a black tunnel. I hear their voices on the other end, riding the waves of darkness. They're muffled. Hushed. They're conversing, but not like the voices you would hear at a normal party. It's almost as if they're speaking in whispers. Maybe they're talking about me? Maybe they're hiding something?

The drizzle is steady outside the house. I can hear it. I'm still in the darkness, waiting, listening as it continues its assault. It's calmed some. The patter has a hypnotic quality to it, and suddenly, quite inexplicably, I feel sleepy. Not sleepy in the usual sense, mind you, but more so tired, that same feeling you get when you've been on vacation for weeks and finally get back home to your own bed. You feel like you could sleep for days on end. That's me right now. If I could, I'd go to sleep for as long as I could. Just lay there in my safe place and dream lovely, blissful dreams.

I begin to walk back toward the sitting room when the house quakes from a crash of thunder. The windows rattle and shudder, the foundation creaks and groans. A few seconds after, a blaze of white explodes, revealing a room I didn't see before.

The voices in the other room go silent.

They're listening, too. I know it.

Two more consecutive pulses of light illuminate the detour a few steps ahead. Curiosity overtakes me, and I steel myself, expecting anything at this point.

I suck in a deep breath, then quickly step out into the entrance to the room.

And standing there, in the threshold, my skin prickles and the itch in my arm comes screaming back, because what's in front of me, is my own death.

A man stares back at me from across the room. He's a silhouette juxtaposed against the storm beyond. His eyes are two black slots. They burn into me. I can feel them, agonizingly intense. He doesn't move, doesn't even appear to breathe. Just waiting.

I can't move, can only stand there frozen in the doorway. I'm not breathing either, mind you. I can't. It's like a lead weight is crushing my chest. My lungs are floundering like two dying fish, slimy and useless.

There's an infinitely loud *CLICK!* and it feels like the sun is right there in front of me. Only there's no heat, but rather a cold, buzzing air. I gasp and twist away as if I've seen some grotesquery, nearly blinded after only seeing a world of darkness for the last hours of my life.

"Are you all right?" a voice asks.

I slowly open my eyes to find that the man across from me isn't a man at all, but rather a rusted copper statue, something designed to look as though it's from the past *and* the future. Fashioned of metal ribbons with dozens of cogs and gears; someone clearly put a lot of care into its construction.

"Do you like it?" the voice repeats.

I turn to find Bernard standing beside me, almost as if he's appeared out of thin air. His glasses rest on the end of his nose, like an old librarian. He shuffles forward and his eyes drift over the sculpture, carefully inspecting it. Admiring it.

"What is it?" I ask.

Bernard turns back to me. His eyes flicker in my direction so fast I almost miss it, and then he turns back to the statue. "One of the Copper Men." His voice is raspy, worn. He's in his fifties but he sounds older.

"Copper Men?"

He doesn't say anything, only nods.

It's then that I see that the copper man isn't the only strange thing in this room. Strewn about the space are multiple elaborate glass displays, with bizarre decorations mounted higher on the walls (most of which are lost in the shadows). It reminds me of a trophy room, only there are no animals. No elephants, or lions. No bears or cheetahs or buffalo heads. No tigers.

There are multiple pedestals checkered around the room with glass cubes on the tops. I look to the nearest and see a simple pair of black eyeglass frames resting on a velvet pillow. In another, a plain watch with a leather band and a crack like a bolt of lightning running through the face. If it wasn't obvious the timepiece was broken, I'd attempt to read the time.

The objects get stranger the further I look. A porcelain doll-like mask with a demented smile bearing a mouthful of needlepoint teeth. And beyond, there's a dynamically posed female mannequin, like some old war hero wearing a red hooded sweater and a pair of torn jeans and black Converse sneakers. The clothes are filthy, with dark stains spotted over the fabric. My mind instantly jumps to Ivy's gown, soaked with blood, her hands held out in front of her in shock. I close my eyes and wish the memory away, imprison it in the vault locked deepest in my mind.

I hone my focus back on the room. Everything here appears to be so random yet so familiar, and I decide not to make any more of a mess of my mind than it already is. Because these things don't fit into any category, they can't be put into the drawer in my mind where rational things belong.

"Beautiful, isn't he?" Bernard asks from behind me. His attention hasn't left the copper man.

I can't think of anything to say, so I just say, "Yes." I'm not lying. It *is* beautiful. There's something about the Copper Man that is precious, like an old toy you'd find buried in the dirt. Something nostalgic that you don't want to let go of.

Bernard, arms folded behind his back, turns to me, rocking on his heels. "Incredible, the things they've discovered."

"Discovered?" I repeat. "What do you mean?

Someone didn't build it?"

I expect Bernard to laugh at my question, but he doesn't. Instead, his eyes narrow a little and he looks at me over the top of his glasses. "*Someone* did." This sounds ambiguous when he says it, like he isn't quite sure himself who created it.

He takes a step closer, like he's sizing me up. Seeing what I'm made of.

"I guess I have your father to thank for it. For all of it," he says, nodding his head at the displays. He's speaking broadly of the contents of the room, of every single hideous little artifact and oddity in these little cubes and on the walls.

"You know my father?"

"Of course." Bernard nods. "Quite well, in fact. His organization has been very generous over the years."

Father was always very generous with money, just not with his time.

"He's come across many remarkable things, hasn't he?"

While he waits for an answer, I only look on at the

Copper Man. I fantasize, thinking about what he would be like if he were alive, and a small smile plays at the corners of my mouth. I think he would be kind, and jolly. He'd be a good, loyal friend, unlike so many things that are for all intents and purposes, "alive."

Bernard continues. "Fortunately for me, your father has little interest in most of the things he finds. He's not one for possessions, your father. Is he?" This is rhetorical.

He's not wrong. Father possessed little sentimentality, if any at all. He didn't keep birthday cards, or ticket stubs. Didn't hesitate to throw things away during spring cleaning. Whatever a hoarder was, he was the exact opposite. A minimalist, if you will. But not for the sake of being a minimalist, but rather a victim of circumstance.

Just like me.

The dining room is a hole in the earth. Literally. It's recessed, sunken. There's a flight of steps we had to take to get down here. The wood paneling is stained so dark it's nearly black. The ceiling arches overhead like a cathedral, and there's a medieval iron chandelier dangling over the center of the room. The décor makes me cringe and I open my fists to find my nails have dug into my palms so badly they're bleeding. I slip my hands onto my lap and hope nobody notices.

The dining table is dramatically long. There are candles tracking down the surface like the lights on a runway. It reminds me of the tables my father would use for conferences and board meetings. There's so much space between each person that it's almost as if we're in different hemispheres. Comical, in a way. I imagine us having to shout to each other to be able to speak, but I quickly find out that's not the case when Bernard begins sharpening a slicing knife for the turkey. Ten pounds of roasted bird rest on a platter surrounded by chopped carrots and potatoes. The scrape of the metal surfaces echoes all around us, vibrating the glass of water in front of me, and I can't keep my teeth from biting down. I imagine them beginning to crack, exposing the nerves and rot within like the soil that's seeped into a casket after being buried for thirty years.

Bernard sets down the sharpener and picks up the boning knife, clumsily wielding the two blades.

His hands shake as he poorly attempts to carve into the turkey. The first cut he makes is pathetic, lopping off an uneven cut of meat while also managing to tear the golden-brown skin away from the rest of the turkey.

The others watch uncomfortably as he fumbles the utensils, the blistering silence bloating the unease in the room.

Finally, George can't take it anymore. He clears his throat and looks at Bernard.

Bernard smiles unevenly, admitting defeat. "A bit out of practice, I'm afraid."

George takes the place of Turkey Carver and Bernard takes his seat. George has done this before. Carved many turkeys in his lifetime. I can tell. Father did, too. He excelled in everything he did, and he took pride in the simple everyman's tasks.

Christmas was more a ritual than a holiday for us. Family events resembled a wake more than an actual holiday celebration. It makes me sad, thinking back and wondering what other families were like at Christmas. The closest I ever came to seeing this was an old black and white film where the family was all smiles and laughs. I remember looking down at the carving knives that night. Father always carved the turkey. That was just how it was in our house. But as the years went by and I had grown, I realized that I never questioned these unspoken rules, never asked *why* things were the way they were. I couldn't. And that's the whole point. There never was a second that I was afforded the opportunity to ask him, or my mother. And when there was, I already knew that any question I posed would just fall on deaf ears. That any query I had would never be answered without contempt, or disdain.

And as I sat there with Ivy at the dinner table, the blades shimmering under the overhead light, I saw something in the reflection of those blades that was magical. Like a whole other world lived in that reflection, and *he* was the only one who got to experience this special thing and nobody else ever could. Looking back, I don't know what came over me.

Father had been in the kitchen. He'd gone to get a bottle of wine while Mother searched for candles. When he'd walked back into the room, he was horrified. Mother froze beside him; I think she was afraid of what he might do. I remember her face. It was panicked, like my father had suddenly transformed into a dangerous wild animal that could kill us at any moment if we made a sound. I'd never seen her so scared or him so angry.

You see, when you live in a house of indifference, micro-expressions are all you have, and there's always resentment blistering below the surface. Father's face didn't have many wrinkles, because his face was always the same. He didn't get angry or sad like other people. He just sort of "was." But when he walked into that room on Christmas Eve, there was a change. Something I'd never seen until that day, then never saw again. I think that was the first time he ever really saw me as more than a daughter. And I use the term "daughter" loosely. In one fell swoop I'd become more than that. I'd become someone who had gotten in his way, who'd decided that I'd had enough of his bizarre rituals and excessively strict tradition. A variable he could no longer control.

By refusing to conform to his rules any longer, I'd suddenly become the enemy. The simple act of cutting the turkey wasn't simple at all to him, but rather a sacred ritual, a responsibility reserved purely for the head of the household. And by taking this from him, I'd disrupted his entire way of being, created an alternate reality than the perfect one he kept in his head.

His eye twitched as he stood there, the bottle of wine in one hand, the corkscrew in the other, disappointment etched into his face. Or maybe it wasn't disappointment at all. Maybe it was plain old simple rage.

I remember it all so clearly. I didn't make anything of it at the time, but he set the corkscrew and bottle on the table and looked at his watch as if reminded of something.

That was the precise minute the old grandfather clock at the end of the hall decided to ring out, chiming over and over again.

We locked eyes while my mother stood there in shock and then I turned and noticed Ivy was standing beyond the red door. Her face looked miserable and scared and I felt my heart break in that moment.

Father began moving toward the red door, toward Ivy, and I quickly stood up from my chair and he froze.

I met Ivy with a look that said, *I'm sorry*. Because I was sorry. Sorry I couldn't be there for her. Couldn't help her get through whatever was happening beyond that red door. And most of all, sorry that I was powerless to do a single thing about it.

Father stood in the entryway to the basement and took one last look at me, then slammed the door so hard the wine bottle fell off the table and shattered on the kitchen floor.

He never cut the turkey again.

The entire table is nervous. I can't pinpoint why, but I can tell by the energy in the room that my hosts are on edge. Everyone keeps their eyes trained on their food as they cut and chew. Like beaten dogs. Cut and chew. The occasional swallow and gulp of wine.

I haven't taken but two bites of mine. The meat looks dry, unappetizing. The rolls look like sandy clogs of dried mud, the potatoes like petrified bits of wood.

The only sounds in the room are the chewing, and the silverware working across the ceramic plates. The reverberation is dreadful. The dining hall would have done well as a music room. Excellent acoustics. So good that I can nearly hear Wilda's pulse in the chair next to me.

I decide that now is the perfect time to break the silence. "So how exactly do you know Officer Smith?"

The cutting stops. I hear the knives slide off the ceramic. All eyes are on me.

"Officer Smith?" Hildy says.

My nervous smile begins to sag, then I say, "He never told me his name. When we met, I mean."

The others glance at each other, as if they've got a secret between them.

George lifts his chin, casually reaching up and thoughtfully twisting the end of his mustache. "Met him when we got to town, same as you."

"He's a very nice man," Hildy adds. As she says this her tone drops, as if she's embarrassed to have remarked on the matter. She collects herself, then smiles politely. "Been working himself half to death, driving around all hours of the day."

"A strange career path," George says. "Doesn't seem like he has the nerves for it."

"Especially in these conditions," Bernard says under his breath.

"He's doing the best he can. After all, someone has to do it, don't they?" Wilda defends. "I only wish there were ten more of him."

I say, "I don't know why. Nothing exciting's ever happened here before. Can't imagine much has changed."

Their voices and chewing trail off into silence, as though they can't believe what I've just said. Like I've spoken blasphemy.

"Like nothing's changed?" Bernard begins to say curiously. He tilts his head down and looks at me over the top of his glasses in that way he does.

"And what exactly is that supposed to mean?" Wilda snaps.

Apparently, I've stirred the hornet's nest.

George holds his hands up defensively, trying to calm the riled strangers. "Now, now, I'm sure that's not what the girl meant. Surely, she knows just as well as any of us how much things have changed. Perhaps she's referring to the 'look' of the town itself?" He smiles, shifting to me to reaffirm this. "You said you lived in Silvers Hollow when you were younger, yes?"

I nod. "It's the same, but…" I timidly tuck a loose strand of my hair behind my ear like I'm a little girl again sitting at a table of grownups, which is an odd feeling for me. I'm used to speaking in front of people, I've done it forever. "This town… It's not how I remember it. Not really. There's just something…*different* than I remember."

Wilda coughs up a laugh like some sort of mummy. "I should think so; how many decades has it been since you've seen it?"

I sigh, pushing the turkey around on my plate with my fork. "I guess it's been a while. I'll admit, it is strange being back home. Everything just looks so…*new*."

"Why wouldn't it?" Bernard says, puzzled. "Look new, I mean. Your father was adamant about maintaining things around here. He's spent millions. The paint. The lights. He's kept everything immaculate. Preserved every last detail."

George straightens in his chair and says, "He's right. Some of these smaller towns are rotting to the core. Mold and grime. Disgusting. They get so goddamn old, people forget they're even there. Half the time they disappear right into the forest. But not Silvers Hollow."

Hildy shifts in her seat when she hears this. I watch out of the corner of my eye as she chugs down the rest of her wine in three large swallows. Her lipstick leaves a pair of smudged lips on the rim of her glass.

I set my knife and fork down on the plate in an unintentional cross. "Did you guys hear about that town up north, in Massachusetts?"

"And what town would that be?" Wilda asks.

The question hits me like a brick wall. I'm tunneling away at memories with torn fingernails, endeavoring to unearth where I'd heard this.

They're right. What town?

It's there in my mind's eye. I can see it through the fog and gray but can't make out the name. "How funny," I say. "I can't remember the name. It's right on the river. Some small fishing village."

Wilda grunts, then begins cutting her turkey again.

"They say they saw things, down by the water," I

continue.

"*Who* says?" George asks.

I shrug. "The townspeople. Just rumors, I guess."

Bernard and George's eyes meet. Bernard says, "Maybe, maybe not." He smiles, and I sense a weight behind that smile, as though he's hardly keeping it together. All of them are barely hanging on.

I fold my arms and lean on the table, twisting my neck so hard that it cracks, and the echo is dry. "They were supposed to send a journalist to find out what was going on. Don't know if they ever did."

"My opinion?" Wilda adds, "Cultists. God only knows what the heathens would be doing down by the water."

Ghastly negatives of the blood painted in the alley flicker before my eyes. "Cultists? There were never any reports of cult activity in the area."

"She has a point, Wilda," Bernard says.

I risk a glance at Hildy and see her eyes are closed like she's been overtaken by a migraine. I think the grisly turn the conversation has gone is getting to her.

"Hildy?" I say. Hildy looks at me grimly, her mouth pulled into a wire thin line. "Are you all right?"

"She's fine," George interrupts. I glare at him for his insensitivity but he's too self-absorbed to notice.

"As I recall, they *did* send a nice young man there," Wilda adds.

I assume she means to elaborate, but quickly find that isn't the case. "What did he find?"

Silence creeps back over the room. I look at all four of them, waiting, but nobody answers me.

"Bernard?"

"Doesn't really matter, in light of recent events, wouldn't you say?" Whereas Wilda's tone was one of indifference before, she's irked now. Something isn't sitting right with her. With any of them.

Doesn't matter? Why on earth wouldn't it matter? Reports pouring in of strange things in the river and floods and they're not the least bit concerned about it. I'm not up for "Humanitarian of the Year" by any means, but I do care about people. At least, I thought I did. I feel my heart twist inside my chest as if it were skewered.

Suddenly a rush of alarm is breezing past me like a train. I hear that familiar heavy whirl in my ears, gigantic fan blades, and a horrible question is whispered to me.

What have you done?

I can't get the thought to leave. But I don't know why it's there, don't understand what it means. I file it away for now and let the door slam closed. I try and shake it off. I have to focus.

I remember seeing the report on the news one night. It was late. I was at the hotel, sitting on the end of the bed in my embroidered robe and slippers, eyes wide open yet much too heavy, half asleep, half awake.

And then there it was.

People were acting more like it was a joke, poking fun at the illiterate fishermen and the ignorant country folk. People dismissed them, writing them off simply because of how they looked. It still makes me angry to this day, the lack of understanding. The judgment that comes so easily and automatically. Like it's a reflex, no harder than breathing. It made me wonder, if it had been me up there, would they have taken the claims more seriously? Would they have heard my voice? Heeded my words? Is there really something there, waiting in the water after dark? It disturbs me, knowing that I'll never find out. Knowing that I never did anything to help those frightened people, the same way I never helped Ivy.

"But aren't any of you afraid?" I say. "Those people are terrified, and Silvers Hollow is so close to…"

It's then that I see they're all staring at me as if I've gone insane, and just as my voice trails off in the cavernous space and silence settles over the dining hall, they erupt into fits of cackling, mad laughter.

After dessert, we retreated to the parlor. It's a sophisticated spot. Shelves of oiled leather books and leather couches.

Leather everything, really. I wonder how many cows died to decorate this fancy room, and my stomach begins to fold in on itself.

George, sitting in an adjacent club chair, lights the end of his pipe and takes a long drag, anxiously unfolding a newspaper in front of him.

Across from him, Wilda crochets a lavender shawl. I can tell that she's inexperienced at this; some of the slip stitches are all wrong, and the yarn is a jumbled mess, but

I don't correct her. Mother taught me on one of the rare occasions when we spoke, and I'd do it every so often growing up, to pass the time. I tried to teach Ivy, but she lacked the dexterity and hand-eye coordination. She worsened over the years, growing pale, with a redness around her eyes. Frail. Crocheting was just another means of escape to me. I even fashioned an entire blanket for Father, but he never used it. To this day I don't know what happened to it.

Hildy looks past me, out the elongated front window overlooking the courtyard. I turn and look over my shoulder and it's like looking at space. A black, endless vacuum that's as harsh as it is cold. The others hide it well, whatever is bothering them, but Hildy isn't as good of an actress. I can see that whatever is wrong is affecting her on a deeper level. She can't preoccupy herself the way the others can, can't force herself to compartmentalize this fear that's in the room with us.

A door groans and Bernard appears from the hall, carrying a polished silver tray with four coffee cups placed on saucers. They look like something reserved for royalty.

Like dishware you'd find in the Royal Palace, or a castle chiseled into the Carpathian Mountains.

The sterling dishes rattle as Bernard sets the tray on the table, and we all breathe a little easier once the rattling stops.

"Has he called?" Hildy quickly asks Bernard. There's an urgency in her voice.

Bernard carefully hands her a refreshment, shaking his head. "No. Not yet. I'm sorry."

I see a chance and seize it. "Wait, you have a phone? Can I make—"

"For in-town calls only," George says dully. "It won't reach outside the city."

"What do you mean?" I say, looking around at the others, "why not?"

George lowers his newspaper enough for me to see his eyes. "The emergency."

I scoff audibly and nobody seems to notice.

"Shouldn't he have called by now?" Hildy says. "Didn't he say he would call?"

Wilda's face softens, and she puts a hand on Hildy's

shoulder. "Try not to worry."

Who in God's name are they talking about? Are they expecting someone else other than the stranger sitting before them on the couch?

"Who?" I ask.

Bernard looks at me, then at George. George hesitates, then nods over the top of his newspaper.

"He's late," Bernard says. "We're waiting on his call, for instructions."

Now I see. They're talking about Officer Smith.

I ask, "Are you expecting him?"

"Yes."

I don't know why, but before I know it, I'm doing exactly what Officer Smith told me not to. Maybe to show him he has no power over me. That I'm the one in control.

"We saw blood," I say. "He saw it, too—Officer Smith," I pause. "I mean the policeman, whatever his name is."

Wilda stops crocheting. George's newspaper slowly falls below his face. Bernard comes away from the window, sinking onto the edge of one of the empty club chairs. Even the howls of the storm seem to get choked off. I didn't mean to alarm them. I really didn't. It was just the first thought that popped into my head and I couldn't even process it before it left my mouth.

Hildy's posture has tightened, her back is straight as a board. George has his hands folded on his lap.

"There was blood? Where?" Bernard asks.

"When I was in town, in one of the alleys behind the church. There was something on the wall. Some sort of symbol. It was... I didn't recognize it." I think about telling them about the tiger, but I don't. Maybe it's because I don't trust them. But even despite this, whether I like it or not, this is the longest conversation I've had with anyone here aside from Dr. Snow.

Bernard looks apprehensively at George, and then at Wilda and Hildy. He takes a deep breath, reaching up and taking his glasses off. "That means that they're here."

I see them begin to drown, to fall apart like wet paper. I turn to Hildy and see two long tears streak down her face, but I don't know why.

"Who's here?" I ask.

It happens in an instant. There's this sound outside, a colossal boom accompanied by rolling shrieks of static, like something electrical has gone haywire. The earth jolts and the windows crash violently. The power cuts out and I'm left in a dark house, the strangers before me transformed into inky shapes.

I hear George's newspaper crumple as he staggers from the chair. A mug hits the carpet and spills. Bernard is on his feet in an instant, attending to Wilda and Hildy.

I jump up equally as fast, steadying myself on the club chair, and make my way to the window. I turn back but see nothing, only hear them all panicking behind me. I look back to the window but I can't make out anything outside either, from inside the house. I feel along the wall to the front door. As I press down with my thumb on the latch, the door explodes open, slamming into the wall so hard a small framed mirror falls off and detonates on the tile.

The noise is incredible. Blood pumps hard in my ears, and I feel lightheaded as the hiss climbs louder yet. Before I can get in a single thought, my clothes are soaked. Water dumps from the black sky and I notice that it's collecting in the courtyard, forming pools, slowly flooding. And it's then that I see it.

The path I took to get to the house is underwater.

A gunshot goes off.

Even amongst the bedlam outside, I hear it loud and clear. My heart seizes completely, and I startle so badly that I stumble into the porch wall.

My ears are ringing, my head spinning, overloaded by my quivering new world. I force myself to take a moment to get my bearings back, stealing a glimpse at the ever-flooding courtyard. I can't help but be reminded of Father and his obsession with time. I imagine giant minute and hour hands under the water, spinning around like an immense doomsday clock.

Another *BOOM!*, deep and powerful, and I nearly

collapse right there on the porch in shock. Parts of me cease functioning; my limbs lock into place and I will them to start. I look back at the entrance to the house and recoil from another deafening blast. The flash lights up the darkness back inside the house.

I look back at the courtyard, watch rivulets of rain pour from the darkness in the sky. I contemplate leaving, just running away as fast as I can. Out of this house. Out of this town. Out of my own head.

But as much as I want to run screaming in the other direction, the small bit of humanity left in me says no. That I've run my whole life and now it's time to stay.

I punch through the darkness into the foyer and my wet shoes slip out from under me. My limbs pinwheel through the air and I crash down on my back and nearly break my hip and arm simultaneously. The back of my skull slaps against the tile and I feel fire bloom again.

For a moment I just lay there, eyes shut, doing everything I can to block out the agonizing pain that's jettisoned throughout my body. As the fire sears my nerves, the noise begins to fade. I feel my soul start to lift from my body and for a single moment I'm alone again. Only I'm not alone. Ivy is there. She's just how I remember her, small and frail, and she smiles at me timidly the way she used to. I reach out to take her hand just in time to see her torn away, as if an airlock has been breached and she's been ripped away into outer space.

My eyes open wide and I see George standing over me, a shotgun in his hands, a blank, empty expression on his face.

I'm too stunned to begin to fight for my life, so instead I just lay there, looking up at him, ready to accept my fate.

There's an equal amount of emotional pain in his eyes and I see it. I lock onto that pain and pray that he believes that I still want to live, that whatever has happened to them isn't happening to me.

"Please..."

"I'm so sorry." George gazes idly out at the courtyard and shakes his head back and forth, a great sadness in his voice. "It's too late..."

He begins to raise the shotgun and I see a vision of Ivy's face whirl before me like a kaleidoscope, colorful and vibrant and wonderful. I see her smile and hold it there, use it to protect myself from the horror of what's about to happen.

A grisly scream shatters my perfect reverie, and the blast is so loud that I feel my ears pop and a metallic ringing ricochets inside my head like shotgun pellets.

I hear a weight crumple to the floor like a sack of potatoes, and when I finally open my eyes, I see a spray of blood on the edge of the ceiling above me. Little pieces of pink bone and coils of brain hang plastered to the wallpaper, and immediately I know that this is what is left of George.

Flustered, I painfully lift my head and crabwalk back. I collide with the entry table and a heavy glass ashtray topples over and shatters on the tile.

The sound of the glass breaking snaps me back into the present. In a daze, I manage to push myself to my feet, pinned to the wall. The only illumination is from the storm outside. Flashes of light flicker beyond the windows and I wince at their blinding colors. Orange. Yellow. Blue. White. Red. They're brief but allow me enough illumination to see the scene in front of me.

And it is one of carnage.

N o matter how hard I try to force myself to understand what is happening, I can't. Not anymore than I can understand why a mother would drown her own baby. Why children would throw live kittens off the side of a bridge or light a homeless man on fire.

And I tell myself that there is evil in this world, and it was never meant to be understood. That it just exists, the same as the stars and the planets.

I push through the strobe of the storm, a silhouette moving in front of the brilliant panes through the parlor.

I stop, eyes closed. I can sense that they're there, in

front of me, but I can't bring myself to look. Can't bear to see their new faces.

I smell gunpowder and rain and smoke.

The wind brushes the back of my neck, seductive-like, and my skin prickles and the hairs on my arm stand on end. Despite the chaos, the itch in my forearm seems to have abated.

Maybe it was never really there at all?

I take solace in this one small thing and grab onto it like a tiny branch as I'm being swept downriver. I listen to my hammering pulse in my ears, and my eyes throb and I feel my arm begin to stiffen.

Maybe my arm *is* broken?

I listen to the wind howl, and that electrical cackling rages on outside the safety of the house. It reminds me of a downed power line, the way the wires hiss and sizzle with electricity.

I imagine one of the telephone poles knocked over somehow during the storm, the wires strewn about like black angel hair pasta.

The storm dies down for a mere moment, and I find

the courage to open my eyes.

What I see in front of me, I can never unsee. It's a part of me now, part of who I am.

Bernard appears to be comfortable in the club chair. His arms rest on the sides and his legs are wide. His body leans back the closer to the top of the chair it gets. And I see his throat kicked back as if he's sleeping.

I slowly step around the side of the chair and gasp. The sheer brutality of what is before me shocks me so, and I stagger back into the bookcase.

Bernard's throat meets his jaw, but beyond that, nothing else. The rest of his head looks as though it has been torn completely off by an animal. It's all shredded layers of skin and mucus and blood. His mangled jaw is still attached, though, and I see the remnants of a tongue lolled to the side. I see the fillings on his bottom molars speckled with bright blood.

My chest heaves, I feel it cave in on itself and suddenly I can't breathe. My mouth is bone-dry. My tongue is a sponge. The air in this room is so thin it's almost as if I'm on another planet. I've never had asthma, but if I did, I have a fleeting suspicion I'd be dead right now.

Beyond Bernard, I see Wilda cast in a deep shadow. Still. For a brief, split-second I feel a glimmer of hope being able to discern in the darkness that her head is still intact. I feel that crushing weight on me shift ever so slightly before all hope is lost.

A sheet of indigo lightning brightens the gruesome scene. I see Wilda's incomplete shawl resting on her lap with the crochet hook in her hand as if she'd never stopped threading the yarn.

Her head is like a plant. Whereas Bernard's was completely removed, Wilda's is like more of an eruption. Like a volcano, only instead of a cloud of ash, her bloody, matted hair sticks up in a wild bird's nest, fragments of gray skull and ribbons of brain pasted to her face. I see the horror in her eyes, like she felt what happened to her just a moment longer than she thought she would. Her mouth is contorted in agony, bloody and raw, and it's then that I notice she's bitten off her own tongue.

A rush of overwhelming terror hits me. I spin around and plant myself as firmly as I can. The horror of what's in front of me bubbles up like poison and I violently spew into an oversized vase, emptying my stomach of whatever food is left. The semi digested turkey, the dry rolls, all of it, comes flooding up my throat. The acid burns and I retch so hard I think, quite irrationally, I might have thrown up my guts.

The vomiting drains what little energy I have left, and I sink to the floor, wracked by giant, obnoxious sobs. I notice that I'm sitting in a puddle of blood so big it looks like the red door. The same one Father would take Ivy to and disappear behind for hours at a time. And now that I see the door there, on the floor, I can't unsee it. Just like the dead bodies littered around me, I can't unsee it. I can never erase it from my mind, never be free of the horrible visions of Hildy's sweet face disfigured into oblivion, of Bernard's exposed jaw with his teeth and tongue. My chest heaves as I cry harder, and before long I can't see because I'm crying so hard. I cry because once again I've failed to prevent the loss of life. Failed to help someone that needed me so badly. I resign myself to loss, and curl into the fetal position, wishing for my own death in a pool of blood.

The world has turned upside down. Where there was light, there is no more. Where there was peace, there is chaos. And where there was a dream, there is a nightmare instead.

Silvers Hollow is a tempest. More unstable and volatile the longer I wait. I can hear the earth shift and groan beneath my feet, hear the surrounding mountains as they break apart and collapse under the weight of a secret.

My secret.

If there wasn't an emergency before, there sure as hell is one now. The town plaza is dark. The power outage wasn't just at the mansion, it was everywhere. The sprawling strings of lights are all extinguished, erased from time.

I stand in the center of the plaza in front of the gazebo on the soggy grass. I've cried so much I think I've run out of tears. My throat and chest burn as I search the surrounding buildings in a frenzy, looking for a sign.

"Hello?" I shout. My voice is carried away in hollow resonances, toward the crashing in the mountains beyond town. The blood on my clothes has mostly been washed away by the torrent gushing from the sky. The water grows louder as the pools get deeper. I cup my hands to the sides of my mouth. "Is anyone there? Anybody? Please!"

There are only echoes and ghosts.

Even the Nighthawk Diner has gone dark. I can only see a faint reflection on the glass. The inside of the diner is nothing more than blackness. The lights in there haven't been turned off since the place opened and I feel fear burrow under my skin like tiny earthworms. I frantically scour the streets with my eyes and discover that the alleys are beginning to flood.

I wonder what has become of the tiger. Has it

retreated, escaped from this nightmare?

And just when I think things couldn't possibly get any worse, I realize that everyone has gone. They've left me here in this watery grave. I search my memories, scouring for even just one good thing, but I can't find it. Everything is gone. Even Ivy has left me.

For the first time in my life, I'm truly and utterly alone.

A t this point, I do the only thing I can do.

I go home.

I'm on my street now. I race past the newspaper stand from before, tear down the sidewalk through hurricane-like winds, forcing myself through it all to get back to the only place I can think of. Not even a *safe* place, at that. Just a place I knew once that I know no more.

I dash through the streets as the earth quivers and I nearly lose my balance and slip. I scream as loud as I ever have. Call for someone. Anyone. My cries for help are so shrill I think my esophagus tears and there's fire in my chest.

But nobody answers. I'm only met with more empty windows and gloom-laden houses.

As I round the bend, I find an old police car parked haphazardly in front of our house.

Officer Smith. The way he's parked makes it clear that he was in a hurry. The red light cycles, throwing tides of ruby over the front lawn and the house.

I stand there drenched in the light, relieved beyond belief to find another soul in this wretched place. My heart slows a bit, and I approach the car.

The rain batters the front windshield, and there's already an inch of water creeping up the tires. I can't see inside; but the driver's door hangs open. The sturdy hinge creaks as the door rocks back and forth in the wind.

I carefully move around the side to find the car empty. The shotgun is still in place, though, and the radio is on. Papers are scattered over the passenger seat. I lean inside and twist the dial on the radio but only hear hisses of static.

My hope renewed, I lift my head to find the front door of the house rocking open, beckoning me inside one last time.

I am an ant before this house. It was never really a home at all, I think to myself. It was a prison. A prison of memories and awful things that I want so badly to forget yet can't. I don't recognize it anymore. Don't recognize who I am. Who I've become.

The strobe of red light presses the urgency of the world falling apart around me, and for the first time I think this is the end. The end of the world. The end of everything.

In the sky high above the house, there's an electrical surge of charged energy and I see the expanse light up once more. Only this time, I can make out a shape in that harrowing darkness.

Something massive looms in the sky over Silvers Hollow, miles-long and round and threatening. My eyes fight to distinguish what's there, and I make out starbursts of neon sparks and coils of heat that remind me of the inside of an oven. The ominous form shrieks with electricity and seeing the scope of something so infinitely large brings my terror to new heights.

I gasp and look away as if seeing my own death. I don't want to see. Don't want to know. My head turned away, I spring forward, arms shielding my eyes, and crash into the door, throwing it the rest of the way open.

A succession of powerful, thunderous crashes rattles the walls and the floor, and the room spins. Outside, I hear an ungodly, alien wail, and the command of my anxiety injects a thousand volts into my veins.

Suddenly, I hear someone laughing while clapping slowly at the same time.

I turn to find Officer Smith sitting nonchalantly in the recliner.

He looks up at me and says, "What took you so long?"

Officer Smith appears to be relatively calm in spite of what's happening outside. Like an old Labrador Retriever. He has his revolver sitting on the end table. His mustache is gone completely now, and he looks much younger without it. Nearly ten years younger. His shirt is unbuttoned, necktie askew. He's a mess.

"I wondered if you'd come," he says. As he speaks, his eyes are vacant, as if he's mentally checked himself out from this horrible new world and gone onto a vacation somewhere better. I don't blame him, because the truth is, the reality is horrifying. He's sunken into the chair, like all of the fight has left him and he has nothing left but his own fear. His chest is deflated and his limbs sag.

He sees me eyeing the gun and lets out a dry, forced laugh.

"Don't worry," he says. "I'm no killer. I couldn't even..."

I take a step closer, as if I'm finally seeing this man for the first time. "Who are you—really?"

Officer Smith reaches up and touches his bald lip where his mustache was. His eyes reflect a haunted gleam. He looks at me, then lets out a halfhearted laugh. "Your father thought it might help."

"Help what?"

"The transition," he replies. "You know, seeing someone familiar. I've never even shot a gun before; I'm an actor. And not a very good one at that."

I stand looking at him, and he at me, and we listen to the tempest as it batters Silvers Hollow. Desecrates it. It will soon be a sunken city, a concrete catacomb littered with bodies and debris and blood. The rain has increased at an alarming rate, and by the looks of the streets, the entire town will soon be underwater.

"They're all dead," I say.

He tilts his head up at me, and I see that he's in shock. Scared maybe even more than me.

"I told them about the alley. Even though you said not to. I'm sorry."

Officer Smith sighs and nods his head, swallowing. His eyes dart to the gun and then away, like he doesn't want to look at it.

"Yeah, I know."

The clot of guilt in my heart is overwhelming and my eyes steadily blur. I feel tears pool in my eyes and my hands go to my face as it occurs to me that they're all dead because of me. Because of what I said.

"It's not your fault," he says matter-of-factly. "What's happening now…well, it would have happened no matter what. It was just a matter of when. I think we all knew that, deep down. What happened with them…it was just them taking control of the only thing they had left.

"I tried to—" He pauses, and I see his bottom lip tremble. "I couldn't go through with it. Not like they did.

I wanted to. But I couldn't pull the trigger, you know?" He nearly whispers this last sentence, like it's a secret.

I stand silently, watching him.

"Does that make me a coward?"

Knowing that nothing I say is going to be able to reassure this man, I keep my mouth shut.

Officer Smith stands uneasily and begins buttoning his shirt like he's just finished a lunch break and is going back on duty.

"Wait," I say.

He stops buttoning and straightens his tie instead.

This is my chance to answer the question that's haunted me this entire time, to see what lies beneath the veil. To find out the truth.

"Why am I here?"

Officer Smith smiles out of the corner of his mouth, a quizzical expression hanging on his face. He cocks his head at an angle, bird-like. "You really don't know, do you?"

I shake my head.

His face softens, and I see pity there, and he nods his head in my direction and I realize that I've been standing in front of the red door this entire time. My blood turns to ice and I can almost feel the door's decaying breath on me.

Officer Smith exhales and says, "Everything you want to know is in there." He leans down and picks up the revolver.

I take a step back and he sees this and holds up a hand peacefully, telling me not to worry.

"Your father—he brought you here. He wanted you to see." He pauses, smiling weakly. "To know."

Holding the gun in his quivering hands, he says, "I wanted so badly for this place to be real." As he finishes his sentence, the earth wobbles again and that familiar electrical hiss shrieks at us, two trespassers in Silvers Hollow.

"But it isn't, is it?" he says. "It was a dream. Just one long bad dream." He looks at me, then says, "Ain't that a bitch?"

We both recoil from a clap of heavy thunder, peering out the living room windows, where we're met with a brilliant panorama of lightning. The scope of the storm seems so much more grand from here, and I imagine that the entire world is blanketed in webs of white-hot electricity.

Officer Smith reaches into his uniform jacket and pulls out a shiny, glittering green box, and I recognize it from earlier. The same one that sat on his seat when he first picked me up at the train station.

"Someone left this for you." He gently sets the box on the end table next to the gun, as if it's the most precious thing in the world. "I'm sorry I didn't give it to you sooner."

This is his parting gift. The only thing left that he could possibly give me to help me on this twisted journey.

"Who?" I say, fighting tears back.

"A friend." Officer Smith pops open the chamber on the revolver and spins it like they do in those old western movies before jerking it to the side and slamming it shut.

"There's six shots in here," he says, setting the gun on the end table. "But I think you're only gonna need one."

I t's under my skin. I can feel it. It has been this entire time.

It started out like a little tickle. Like a feather brushing against my arm. It didn't even hurt. Almost felt sort of nice in some strange way.

Then, a little time passed, and it began to tingle, the way your foot does when it falls asleep. Only now, it was in one particular spot.

At first I thought maybe a bug had bitten me. A mosquito. Or maybe a spider. One of those furry brown ones that like to jump off the walls. We'd even seen a black widow once, out in the garage.

Father killed it with a shovel.

I remember getting into bed one cold winter night. I'd stayed up until one in the morning doing a cross-stitch of a rose.

Ivy was nowhere to be seen. By this time, I'd learned not to question her whereabouts anymore. I had changed into my pajamas and folded the covers down to slip into bed, and there it was. Sitting right there on the pillow, like it was waiting for me. Expecting me.

This spider wasn't furry. It wasn't a "friendly" spider. It was dark and wet, and its legs were sharp and long. Like something that scampers out of a nightmare. A shudder ran through me, then, seeing it desecrating my pillow with its spiny legs.

I tiptoed over to Ivy's dresser and grabbed a tissue, and somehow, as if the spider could sense what I was about to do, it scurried away.

I didn't expect it to run. For something so small, it moved unnaturally fast. Like its life depended on it—which it did. I rushed to snatch it up, but it scuttled away into the blankets and sheets.

I had seen a spider—and chased the vile thing right into my own bed.

This tiny, *hideous* thing had made itself a new home in the one place—the only place—I felt a modicum of safety.

But now, it has nowhere left to go. I've finally found it.

I stagger into the kitchen, balancing myself as the world shudders, and jerk a knife out of the butcher's block.

I push up my sleeve and look down at my skin, where my forearm is raw and practically bleeding from all my scratching.

The blade sinks into my flesh easier than I thought it would and there's instant relief. Dark blood oozes up like oil. There's a euphoric feeling as the metal carves through the outer layer and sinks into the layer of fat below and I think back to when I cut the turkey that night and the look on Father's face, and how much easier this feels. How much more natural.

The blade clatters to the floor and I slip my fingers into the blood. The skin pulls apart like rubber and my fingers slide past the nerves and skin, but I only feel the warmth. My fingers probe inside my arm, hot and sticky, and then I feel it brush my fingertips.

I knew it.

I dig deeper, and push apart whatever is there, inside, and then I close my fingertips over it, and it begins to slip away. I watch that same horrible spider scurry into my bed and disappear forever, and my fingers tighten.

I have it.

My fingertips are tiny vices, now, and I don't care how much it hurts. I force the incision open in a spurt of steaming blood and a wave of nausea passes over me.

Head reeling, barely able to stand, I turn my blurry sight down and open my fist.

My entire hand is covered in dark, tacky blood. In the center of my palm, lying in the pool of blood the same way I did no more than an hour ago, is a small coiled shard. The flutters of light from beyond the window shine on it and it sparkles at me.

I've finally found it.

The red door towers over me like some great beast. The red is bright in this bleak new world, and it burns brighter and more brilliant than anything before it.

Officer Smith has gone. He left the small gift box and the gun and walked straight out the front door into the storm. He didn't even bother taking his car, just casually strolled down the sidewalk and disappeared.

I've fashioned a makeshift tourniquet for my arm, but it won't hold forever. The blood is seeping out, slowly draining me of what little energy I have left.

Water pools under my feet, flowing under the red

door like a drain. I can hear it cascading down the cement steps on the other side.

This is the moment I've been waiting for. The chance I should have taken all those years ago. It was too late to help Ivy. I know that now. She can't be saved any more than the people still left in this town. But that notion doesn't deter me from my mission.

I hustle and collect the gift box and the gun, and approach the red door.

A memory of Ivy standing on the other side of the door slaps me like a dead, wet hand. I see her there, with her frightened little face. Her shaking hands. She hugs that old stuffed bunny with the bow on its head pressed to her chest. I can see her there, pleading with her eyes for me to help her, and I remember the stifling fear and guilt in that moment. The powerlessness. It's all too much. The emotions begin to knead together, folding in on themselves over and over again, hardening and forming something volatile.

My heart isn't racing, isn't jackhammering away like before, no. Because for once, it's perfectly and utterly calm for maybe the first time since I arrived here.

I summon the last reserves of my voice and scream, long and splendid. A flash lights up the room and my ears ring as I kick the door as hard as I can, splintering it open in a wooden symphony of destruction.

I stand at the top of the cement steps, gazing down at the pit of darkness. A strong draft escapes past me, and the first thing I think of is a tomb.

My tomb.

There are a million scenarios that play through my mind as I climb down the steps. I try not to lose control seeing grotesque, unspeakable acts of my worst fears being committed in this basement. There's a sick sucking sound as the suction pulls at my steps. The most awful, devastating things I could imagine drift in and out of the transom of my mind. I realize that I've journeyed not only to the darkest depths of the house, but also of my own soul.

Only this time I don't run. I don't turn away and let it happen. I don't let it control me, or define who I am. I face it, head on. Even if it's going to be a head-on collision, it's going to be a glorious one.

I take two final steps down and stumble as my feet sink into a foot of water.

The gun flies out of my hand and is swallowed with a gulp, and the gift box splashes into the still water and loyally bounces back from under the surface. It bobs there for a moment, before being carried away into the darkness.

I sigh, as if all my friends have suddenly abandoned me.

I can't tell how big the basement is, but judging by the water I hear, I assume it's easily the size of the first floor of our house. My eyes narrow, and I wonder what lies beyond the safety of the light, tucked away in the quiet, damp blackness.

I imagine a soiled mattress, soggy and torn, sitting in the corner of the room on the concrete. I imagine iron shackles on the wall with thick black chains and instruments of torture. I remember Ivy standing beyond my bedroom door, her gown covered in lakes of blood, her arms mapped with dark bruises. She looks at me in shock, and then the door slams closed.

I take another step toward the darkness, and I imagine a tripod and a video camera and I imagine Ivy screaming and a wave of nausea comes over me. I feel bile creep up my throat, but I forced myself to swallow it back down. I imagine horrible, awful things in that darkness. The same ones I failed to prevent.

The sound disturbs the glass cage I'm trapped in, and I watch the dreadful images crack and splinter. I'm transported to an ice cave. Deep fissures branch through the ice. I hear it crack and somehow I'm mindful that they run deep, splitting apart the walls around me with such a clear, concise tone, it's almost like otherworldly music.

There's a chirp. Like a giant, digital cricket has just greeted me. I see a blinking red light on the wall next to me, and out of impulse, half-crazed with desperation and the darkest desire for the truth, I reach out and slap the light on the wall.

I hear a second sound, and I imagine a spaceship hatch opening, and on the far wall across from me, a thin, glowing slot begins to rise with the noisy squeal of hydraulics.

A monitor flickers to life. The power is out all over town, but somehow it has been preserved here. There's a heavy *Clack!* as the monitor settles at its final height. The screen struggles to light fully, and there's one final chirp.

Static sizzles from the device as I wade through the water for a closer look, mindful not to get too near where I suspect the atrocities have occurred.

The uproar of the storm is gone. The small screen is the only thing left in the room. The concrete walls are no more. The darkness, and the rushing water. All of it is gone.

The screen goes light, then dark, and just as I think it has gone out and will never turn back on, I hear a charge and the electricity sings and the screen flares to life like a match. And there's a man on the screen, looking at me.

It's Father.

"Hello, my dear."

A second after he says my name, the power in the walls groans to life like a hall of ghosts. A series of overhead lights kick on one after another. Boom. Boom. Boom. Boom.

The light is blinding. Divine, almost. I've never been so happy to see the light before this moment.

As badly as I want to see what's there next to me in the room, finally know the truth of what transpired down here all those years ago, I'm too overcome with emotions to look.

Father watches me from the screen, allowing me to collect myself.

"Father?" I don't recognize my voice.

The man doesn't speak, only watches me, and I quickly realize I'm watching a recording. "Hello, my dear. If you're watching this right now, then we don't have much time." Father looks at me and every muscle inside my body contracts. All of the fury inside of me boils and the color drains from the room until all that's left is red.

The message continues to play like a commercial as I stand in a room that is slowly being submerged. If I stay much longer, I'll drown.

"I know that you are angry with me. And I know you have questions. Questions you want answered. But we have very little time. And as I taught you so well, time is precious."

I wade through the slush until I'm mere feet from the monitor. I reach out, and my fingers trace his face on the screen. It's surreal, seeing him like this.

"Your mother and I intended to be there with you, but that proved to be impossible in light of recent events." He pauses, reflecting on what he's said, then says, "The Event. That was what the media called it. You were in Winterview that night. It was…" his voice trails off. "Afterward, very bad things started happening. They were subtle changes at first. Decreases in temperature. Leaps in barometric pressure. Electrical storms. Floods. New species washing up on the shore. Before long, those were the least of our worries. There are…" Father pauses, and I relish seeing him frightened the way I'd seen Ivy frightened so many times before. "*Horrible things* have come. And now, the world is unrecognizable. I fear it shall be over soon—for all of us. I know; you're confused. You don't remember any of this. Truth is, you never do. Ever since the accident—"

The image cuts out along with my answers. My body goes rigid and my other palm slams on the cool glass.

There's a hiss of static and the image brightens and Father's voice comes back, distorted at first, then clear.

"—haven't been the same since," he says. "The damage to the hippocampus was…irreparable. Somehow, you still retain fragments. But to you, they're more like dreams.

"They kept finding you, out in the streets. Wandering in the dark. Alone. Your mother and I were so worried about you." Liar, I think to myself.

Father continues. "The implant in your arm; that was for our peace of mind. I thought it might be easier to keep track of your movements." My eyes drift to the blood-soaked rags pasted to my forearm. "What choice did we have? We couldn't lock you up in a cell like some animal. And Silvers Hollow—we thought it was the safest place for you.

"But I guess we were wrong, weren't we?" he says. Father's tone hardens and his callus demeanor returns. "I was made aware of the situation there, in Silvers Hollow, less than twenty-four hours ago. Due to circumstances beyond my control, I was unable to prevent what's transpiring there, and now I fear the worst for you and the others still left in Silvers Hollow.

"Time has *finally* run out." Father bows his head and then looks back up and his piercing gray eyes meet my own. "To that end, I think it only fair that you know the truth."

Up on the surface, something collides with the earth and the impact knocks open the light fixtures on the ceiling. Father bleeps to a black screen again while fluorescent bulbs meet the walls and shatter into dust, the others swinging and dropping into the water in front of me with small splashes. But a select few remain in place, and now I finally see the room for what it is.

My breath hitches and I scrub water out of my eyes with my knuckles, because I can't believe what I'm seeing. In none of the scenarios that reeled in and out of my most frightening, dangerous thoughts did I ever picture what's really here.

I've made a terrible mistake.

The walls aren't cement at all. They're not dusty, stained concrete.

They're the opposite. White. Sterile. Sleek.

Along the perimeter of the room are all manner of scientific and research equipment. Microscopes. Vials. Blood samples. There are even several long, coffin-shaped machines upright along the walls with two-inch thick cables disappearing into the wall.

I splash forward, and my hands run over the various apparatuses placed in front of me. I fumble a few of them, knocking over the glass instruments as the screen flickers back to life.

A lab.

This titanic secret locks the missing pieces together inside my head and everything becomes razor-sharp and vivid. All of the fogginess that's been trapped inside my head dissipates and I can see clear again. My entire foundation rocks, and tremors shoot up and down my arms and legs, only this time it isn't from whatever is happening outside.

The change is inside me. Happening from within.

Father reappears on the monitor and I hear his voice break through the static. "Ivy was ill since the day she was born," he says solemnly. "A rare, congenital heart defect."

A little bit more of the floor drops away under me and an emotional dam brings hundred-foot waves crashing down. Thousands of gallons of water flood in, becoming my new reality. I fall to the floor on my hands and knees, half of me in the freezing cold water, the other half struggling to breathe.

"This room looks exactly as it did all those years ago. Identical down to the tiniest detail, the same as the day you left. You wanted so badly to know what went on down here, but I could never bring myself to tell you. Because saying it out loud, saying the words…that would only make it more real. And I couldn't bear the thought of hurting you anymore than I already was. Every time I looked at you, I saw her, dying right here in my arms."

I turn my head toward him and see that he's in pain. I was wrong about him. He couldn't run forever or shut out his emotions completely. They've slowly eaten away at him, softened the lines in his face. How is this possible?

"Don't you see? Everything that your mother and I did, was for the greater good. To save her. To keep our family together. To keep Ivy alive."

A speeding train twenty cars long plows into me in an unparalleled revelation, and I finally understand his obsession with time. It wasn't a hobby, or something to entertain or busy himself with in his spare time; I'd completely misunderstood. He was fixated on time because he knew that every minute that he wasn't trying to save Ivy's life was a minute lost. That every second on his watch could be the last that he saw her breathe, or smile.

I look up at the monitor and see someone else looking

back at me.

A stranger.

The same as the rest of the people I've met on my journey back to Silvers Hollow. This isn't the same monster I'd lived with growing up. He wasn't some twisted, nightmarish caricature. He was a human being so deeply broken by his own powerlessness to help his children that he couldn't stand to live with himself anymore.

The barriers he put up were his way of protecting himself from the pain, of rationalizing the time he needed to rest, because doing anything but trying to save Ivy, to him, was unacceptable.

I think back, listening to him speak to me from the screen. I begin tearing through my memories, watching him steal glimpses at his watch, or looking up at the clock on the wall to check the time during dinner. He didn't do it because he was anxious to be rid of us. He did it because he loved Ivy so much and he was literally watching her die. An emotional cancer that robbed him of his humanity.

So he pushed her away.

Pushed me away.

Put all of us at a distance, so no one could ever get close to him. Because he knew that one day, Ivy would slip through his fingers, just like she did.

Father's message ends like a candle being snuffed out, and I'm left staring at a blank screen.

In my stupor I peer around the room. The water is ice, waist-high now. I question if there's any point to leaving this room. That maybe I should just die here, in this clean room.

I feel a playful tap on the back of my hip and twist around.

It's the foil gift box. It bumps me like an impatient pet, caught in the current spilling down the staircase.

I reach down and pluck the shimmering thing from the water.

There's only one question left to answer.

The green is absolutely breathtaking. It sparkles at me, this elusive, almost mystical object. Maybe it's just me. Maybe it only looks so perfect and delightful because of all the ugly things I've seen tonight.

I have it placed in the center of the kitchen table in front of me but haven't been able to bring myself to open it. I'm shaking. Cold, and wet.

The storm has worsened. Outside, Haunter Drive is littered with debris and remnants of earth. The entire front yard is underwater, along with portions of the road. The interior of the house isn't much better. The devastation makes me wonder how far this goes. Is it only Silvers

Hollow that will be wiped from the maps?

I'm only able to subdue my panic by telling myself that there is no way I can possibly escape at this point.

But is that really the truth?

I pick up the box and pull the ribbon. It unfurls, silky and smooth. I carefully set it down on the table like a wounded bird and lift the lid. The cardboard square comes off so easily in my hands it's like it's meant to be.

My eyes go wide as I behold what's inside.

Sitting there on a small cotton tuft is a miniature helicopter. Metal. Aged gold.

I reach in and pick it up, feel its weight. The instant I caress the cool metal between my fingertips, something electrifying happens. A bolt of lightning webs throughout my body, exploding through my blood and muscle and bone and charging them in a sensation I've never known before. And then, I know.

Father isn't the villain in this story.

I am.

The terrible truth plays out in intense glimpses of the past, of what led me to Silvers Hollow.

To *this* moment.

I'm in a helicopter in Winterview City, looking down on a sea of madness. The whirr of the blades, the smell of burning diesel. Everything falls into place.

I feel heat, and flames. Panic, and fear. There's an alarm shrieking, and smoke. I see people running in all directions, screaming. Children crying. Cars mowing down bodies as they flee. It is true and absolute carnage.

What's happening in Silvers Hollow is because of me. People trusted me. They came here because I told them they should. They listened to me, and now, they run screaming for their lives.

I feel the world spin out of control in abrupt, jerky movements. The smoke sears my throat and lungs and I retch and choke. Glass explodes in a thousand exquisite diamonds and there's a heavy metal grind, like a lawnmower blade cutting through an overgrown thicket.

I was the one who invited this chaos, encouraged it at the behest of my father and his company. I brought them all here with my words. All of these people.

I see a shower of blood, and a doomed red sky pinned

with bodies like black stars.

I'm as much to blame as he is.

A sinking feeling begins to rise in my chest, just like the one drowning this town. I feel it slowly swallowing my heart and soul.

As the alarm screeches, my knuckles white, fingertips dug into the leather, the realization hits me that this helicopter crash will savage my mind and eventually lay waste to all of my most precious memories.

I see their faces—Ivy, Father, Mother, Officer Smith, Hildy—in the crowds below, looking up at me as the helicopter tailspins out of control. My vision swims and the world whirls faster and faster as I plummet to the earth.

And I land right here, in Silvers Hollow.

It was me. I am the woman in the shadows.

And then everything stops.

The visions.

The chaos.

And then time itself.

Tears are streaming down from my face. My body feels light; like I could just float away like a balloon.

Hundreds of people are dead because of me. I led them all to their deaths. Every. Last. One of them.

And miraculously, all of the seemingly extraordinary problems I had an hour ago don't seem so extraordinary anymore. Because after finding out the truth, I grasp that it was all in my head.

I'm not powerless. I never was. I only thought I was. All I ever had to do was act. It's all I've *ever* needed to do.

My fingers close around the helicopter, and I hear Father whisper one final riddle in my ear.

"A woman is trapped in a room. The room has only two possible exits: two doors. Through the first door, there is a room constructed from a magnifying glass. The sun instantly incinerates anything or anyone that enters. Through the second door, there is a dragon that breathes fire. So, how does the woman escape?"

Night.

It's been the answer all along. Every bizarre moment and blood-soaked memory I have hits me like a shower of bullets.

I'm underground. That's why it's always dark. Because the sun is hidden away, maybe miles above me.

I rush outside and stumble down the porch steps and through the rain into the pool that is our front yard. Electricity sings and destruction bellows and I look to the darkness, and I face it.

The blackness starts to pull away, and I watch the colossal object hovering in the sky come into focus.

The longer I watch the display of lights, the longer I see that this isn't what I thought it was at all. My eyes follow the shape to the edge and I see that there are dozens more.

I don't know exactly what they are, but they're malfunctioning, damaged from the catastrophe. I surmise they must be something for regulating artificial light, and weather. Gigantic machines meant to simulate rain and wind, and cycles of day and night. I try and fathom what sort of cavern would be big enough to fit an entire town inside, and I think back to the tiger, and the moths.

This isn't Silvers Hollow. It never was. If I'm where I think I am, I'm not even in the same country. What this place *is*, is Father's end game; his tasteless rendition of a fallout shelter. Only it's painfully evident that this refuge will never withstand whatever it is meant to withstand. He's failed to save me just as he failed to save Ivy.

That dog wasn't Bob. And his peculiar behavior suddenly makes sense. No wonder he acted so funny; he wasn't my dog. Just some imitation. For a fraction of a second I wonder where he's gone and part of me hopes he has escaped, but the world begins shaking again and the thought is gone as quickly as it came.

I look around, take in the rising water and the mysterious dark world I've been wandering around all night. I think of a snow globe again, imagine myself inside, trapped.

A fresh wave of devastation hits me and I feel my soul being ripped out.

I think back to my drive with Officer Smith, think about how he watched the river, and I remember the unease on his face looking at that water. Because he *knew*. He knew that the river hadn't been there an hour ago. And he knew that if the water level had raised as much as it had in that short a time, there was a leak.

And the rain.

This isn't rain at all. The cavern is collapsing, and the bleakness of this situation somehow becomes substantially worse. The water must be coming from the surface. And this fake, evil little town will slowly be wiped from the earth and turned into a sunken hollow.

I'm going to drown to death.

This is the emergency. How did I not see it this entire time, as the world unraveled before my eyes? The "emergency" was just their codename for what's been happening. The collapsing cavern, the flooding, the malfunctioning machines. All of it.

Despite what's happening, I feel better, knowing that this was never the town I grew up in. That the only good memories I had with Ivy won't be swallowed up by the water and earth and darkness. That the true Silvers Hollow is still out there somewhere. That the blue, glistening sapphire paint hasn't been changed.

I think about my life. About Ivy. About how every preconceived notion I've ever had about Father has been wrong. About all the people I guided to their deaths. And I scream inside knowing I can never right those mistakes.

I wade through the water and the magnificent ruin, and the entire earth shudders. I lose my balance and everything goes chilled and numb and muffled. I thrash, flailing my limbs, and find my footing. I push myself out of the water and hear something in the sky groan like a mammoth ship arriving to port. There's a sound like metal giving way and then a whistle.

The end is near. I can feel it. The colossal mechanisms on the ceiling of the cave are breaking free and sailing to the earth and leveling the town, one at a time. I see each one sluggishly tear free from what I can only assume are steel support beams. I see a shower of sparks behind each of them while they tumble end over end to the earth like gigantic grand pianos. And I think to myself that they're beautiful, like shooting stars.

I explode out of the water and collapse to the street, which is fairing marginally better. The pavement is partially submerged, but still mostly visible. I stagger from the thunderous blows, fighting my way to Officer Smith's car, and do the only thing I can think of—I climb.

Suddenly, I'm a child again. I'm me before it all happened. Before the pain and agony of growing up in a house where I never knew love. Where I was afraid every night, lying in bed. Where fear and time were the only parents I knew.

All of that is gone now.

I seize this second chance, and there is no more

powerlessness, only power. I let go of everything and it feels like poison leaving my body. I am in control of my own destiny.

My hands and feet slip on the wet metal as the water gushes from the sky, and I push off my knees, rising on the roof of the cruiser like a phoenix. Because that's exactly what I feel like.

I am fire.

I am electricity.

I am loss.

I am regret.

But most of all, I am love. I am all the things that I never thought I was, never believed I could be. And I finally find the courage to forgive myself for it all, to let go of who I was. To let go of Mother and Father, and all of my hate and anger and sadness that I've held inside for so very long.

And as I stand there, in that supreme moment, lost in the rain and the storm to end all storms, I feel at peace for maybe the first time in my entire life. The warmth wraps around me like a blanket and I smile.

I turn, and Ivy is there, looking up at me and smiling,

too. She slips her fingers in mine and I squeeze her hand and tell her that I love her. That I'm sorry. And she forgives me. And together, we watch the end of the world.

Far away, hidden among the destruction, I hear the distant sound of a train.

ACKNOWLEDGMENTS

THIS ENTIRE PROCESS HAS BEEN A DREAM, WHICH IS, AS you know, one of the prevailing themes of the story itself. And much like dreams, it's easy to get lost in your work without a little direction. To that end, I'd like to take a moment to thank all of the good folks who contributed something to this novel in one way or another.

Saren Richardson and Julia Lewis. You both helped me edit this book and polish it up to a mirror shine, and it turned out better than I could have ever hoped for.

Ross Nischler, for designing covers that never cease to impress me, something you know isn't easy to do. Thanks, man.

I'd also like to thank my beta readers, who gave me valuable input on what was and wasn't working, and also catching pesky typos. Tali Leonard. Authors Susanne Perry and Briana Morgan for amazing feedback. Michelle

PATRICK DELANEY

Donaldson. Joyce Lara. Michelle Ward. Doctor Moranda. Lili. Mom. Grace Wilson. Celso Hurtado. Brittany Hydorn. All of you guys helped me figure out how to bring out the best experience for the reader, and I'm grateful for you all. Thank you.

A big thank you to Sadie Hartmann and John Langan for blurbing this book. Sadie is one of the most hardworking and dedicated horror reviewers out there, and I'm proud to call her a friend. And John is a treasure not just among horror writers, but writers in general, and a hell of a decent human being. You won't find a nicer guy.

Also, a big thank you to Warner Brothers. The town of Silvers Hollow is my eerie rendition of Stars Hollow (a tribute to my love, who is the biggest *Gilmore Girls* fan you'll find), which was filmed on "Midwest Street" in Burbank, California. We had the pleasure to see it in person on the Studio Tour. Go check it out and you'll be able to see Silvers Hollow (and Stars Hollow) in person. This is worth the price of admission alone. Just don't go at night, and if you do, best not to look up.

And last but not least, an enormous thank you to everyone that reads, reviews, and shares my work. Without you, there would be no point.

Sincerely,
Patrick Delaney (pdred1985@gmail.com)
3/13/19 — 06/12/20

Also by Patrick Delaney

Dante's Town of Terror

Dante's Wicked World

The House that fell from the Sky

ABOUT THE AUTHOR

Author Patrick Delaney is originally from Los Angeles county. He relocated to Northern California in the early 2000s, and wrote his first novel at eighteen. His debut, *Dante's Town of Terror*, was awarded two literary awards, including a Gold Medal from the Independent Publisher Book Awards, and a Bronze Medal from the Readers' Favorite Book Awards. He has published a sequel, as well as a second standalone novel called, *The House that fell from the Sky*.